A Lucy Novel

Lucy's "Perfect" Summer

faiThGirLz!™

2 corinthians 4:18

A Lucy Novel

Lucy's "Perfect" Summer

Nancy Rue

ZONDER**kidz**

ZONDERVAN.com/
AUTHORTRACKER
follow your favorite authors

ZONDERKIDZ

Lucy's "Perfect" Summer
Copyright © 2009 by Nancy Rue

Requests for information should be addressed to:
Zondervan, *Grand Rapids, Michigan* 49530

Library of Congress Cataloging-in-Publication Data
Rue, Nancy -
     Lucy's perfect summer / by Nancy Rue.
       p.   cm. — (What about Lucy? ; bk.3_)
     "Faithgirlz!"
     Summary: Facing up to a cheater at an elite soccer day camp and some
     difficult events at home helps eleven-year-old Lucy do some growing up
     during a summer which, while very different from the one she imagined, turns
     out to be just right.
       ISBN 978-0-310-71452-1 (softcover)
     1. Soccer—Fiction 2. Sportsmanship—Fiction. 3. Christian life—Fiction.
     4. Single-parent families—Fiction. 5. Blind—Fiction. 6. People with
     disabilities—Fiction. 7. New Mexico—Fiction. I. Title.
     PZ7.R88515Lun 2009
     [Fic]--dc22   2008045729

Published in association with the literary agency of Alive Communications, Inc., 7680 Goddard Street, Suite 200, Colorado Springs, CO 80920.
www.alivecommunications.com

Zonderkidz is a trademark of Zondervan.

Art direction & cover design: Sarah Molegraaf
Interior design: Carlos Eluterio Estrada

Printed in the United States of America

09 10 11 12 13 14 • 22 21 20 19 18 17 16 15 14 13 12 11 10 9 8 7 6 5 4 3 2 1

So we fix our eyes not on what is seen, but on what is unseen. For what is seen is temporary, but what is unseen is eternal.

— 2 Corinthians 4:18

1

Dear God: Why My Life Is Just about Perfect

1. School is out for the summer!!!!!!!!!!!

Lucy would have made more exclamation points, but Lollipop, her pot-bellied kitty, was watching from the windowsill above the bed, her black head bobbing with each stroke and dot. She'd be pouncing in a second.

Lucy protected the Book of Lists with her other arm and wrote…

2. Aunt Karen is taking her vacation to some island, so she won't be coming HERE for a while. YES!!

3. I can practice soccer every minute that I want to — which I HAVE to do if I'm going to be accepted to even try out for the Olympic Development Program. Hello — biggest dream on the planet!

4. We have a soccer game on our field in two weeks, thanks to Coach Auggy. A for-REAL game, with a whole other team, not just our team split up, which is always lame since we only have eight players to begin with. I cannot WAIT!!!!!!!!!!!!!!!

Lollipop twitched an ear at the pen.

"Forget about it," Lucy said to her. She'd only just learned the joy of making exclamation points from Veronica, who was a girly-girl, but who did have her good points. Lucy snickered. "Good *points*, Lolli. Get it?"

Lollipop apparently did not. She tucked her paws under her on the tile sill and blinked her eyes into a nap. Lucy slipped a few more exclamation marks in before she continued.

5. I get to hang out with J.J. and Dusty and Veronica and Carla Rosa and Mora any time I want, not just at lunch or soccer practice or church. Okay, so I already got to hang out with them a lot before summer, but now it's like ANY time, and that's perfect. Except we're still stuck with Januarie. If she weren't J.J.'s little sister, we could just ditch her, but she needs a good influence. We're a good influence.

Lucy glanced at her bedroom door to make sure it was all the way shut. The Book of Lists was her private way of talking to God, and everybody else in the house — Dad and Inez, the housekeeper-nanny, and her granddaughter Mora — knew to leave it alone. Still, she always had to figure out whether it was worth risking discovery to write down what she really, really thought. She decided it was and added.

Well, maybe Mora's not that good of an influence.

Besides, God already knew she was thinking it. She'd discovered that if He wanted her to think anything different, He would definitely let her know. She wrote some more:

6. We can go buy little chocolate soccer balls at Claudia's shop in the middle of the day, or have breakfast at Pasco's café or take picnics to OUR soccer field, because — guess what? — It's SUMMER !!!!!!!!!!!!!!!! !!

Something black whipped across the page and Lucy's pen flew into space, landing with a smack against the blue-and-yellow toy chest and knocking down the ruler Lucy always kept there to hold it open in case Lollipop needed to jump in and hide. The lid slapped shut, and Lolli sprang into an upside down U before she leaped and skidded across the top with her claws bared. She glared indignantly at Lucy.

"You did it, Simplehead," Lucy said. "Just a minute. I'll open it for you." But before she could even scramble off the bed, Lolli dove under it. A squalling fight ensued with Artemis Hamm, their hunter kitty, who had obviously been sleeping beneath the mattress.

"Break it up, you two!" Lucy said. But she didn't dare stick her hand under the bed. One of them would eventually come out with a mouth full of the other one's fur, and it would be over.

"What's going on in there?" said a voice on the other side of the door.

Lucy stuck the Book of Lists under her pillow. It was Dad, who couldn't see, but she always felt better having her secrets well hidden when other people were in the room.

"Come on in—if you dare," Lucy said.

She heard Dad's sandpapery chuckle before he stuck his face through the crack. She cocked her head at him, ponytail sliding across her ear. "What happened to your hair?"

He ran a hand over salt-and-pepper fuzz as he edged into the room. "Gloria just gave me my summer 'do down at the Casa Bonita. Is it that bad?"

"No. It's actually kinda cool."

"What do I look like?"

"Like—" Lucy thought for a second. "Did you ever see one of those movies about the Navy SEAL team? You know ... when you could still...?"

"Yeah."

"You look like one of those guys."

"Is that good?"

"That's way good."

Dad smiled the smile that made a room fill up with sunlight. Lucy could have told him he looked like a rock star, and he wouldn't have known whether she was telling the truth or not. But she did think her dad was handsome, even with eyes that sometimes darted around like they didn't know where to land.

He made his way to the rocking chair and eased into it. It would be hard for anybody who didn't know to tell he was blind when he moved around in their house, as long as Lucy kept things exactly where they were supposed to be. She leaned over and picked up her soccer ball, just escaping a black-and-brown paw that shot from the hem of the bedspread.

"Keep your fight to yourselves," Lucy said.

"What's that about?"

"Exclamation points. It's a long story."

"Do I want to hear it?"

"No." Lucy could see in the sharp way Dad's chin looked that he hadn't come in just to chat about catfights. She hugged the ball. "Okay, what? Is something wrong? Something's wrong, huh?"

"Did I say that?"

"Aunt Karen's coming, isn't she? Man! I thought she was going out in the ocean someplace and we were going to have a peaceful summer." She dumped the ball on the floor on the other side of the bed.

Dad's smile flickered back on. "What makes you think I was going to talk about Aunt Karen?"

"Because she's, like, almost always the reason you look all serious and heavy."

"You get to be more like your mother every day, champ. You read me like a book."

"Then I'm right." There went her perfect summer. She was going to have to redo that list.

"But you're in the wrong chapter this time," Dad said. "Aunt Karen's going to St. Thomas."

"He's going to *need* to be a saint to put up with her."

Dad chuckled. "St. Thomas is an island, Luce."

"Oh." She was doing better in school now that Coach Auggy was her teacher, but they hadn't done that much geography this year.

"I just want to put this out there before Inez gets here."

His voice was somber again, but Lucy relaxed against her pillows. If this wasn't about Aunt Karen wanting to take Lucy home with her to El Paso for the summer, how bad could it be?

"So, you know Inez will be here all day, five days a week."

"Right, and that's cool. We get along okay now." Lucy felt generous. "I don't even mind Mora that much anymore."

"I've asked Inez if she'd be okay with Mr. Auggy also coming in to do a little homeschooling with you."

Lucy shot up like one of her kitties when they were freaked out.

"School?" she said. "In the *summer?"*

"Just for a few hours a week."

"Dad, hello! This is summertime. I have a *ton* of work to do to get ready for the soccer game if I want anybody from the Olympic Development Program to even look at me. That's way more important to me than school!"

"You've improved a hundred percent since Mr. Auggy started teaching your class—"

"Yeah, so why are you punishing me by making me do more work? I don't get it."

She wished she could make exclamation points with her voice.

"You'll get it if you let me finish."

Dad's voice had no punctuation marks at all, except a period, which meant "Hush up before you get yourself in trouble." Lucy gnawed at her lower lip. She was glad for once that he couldn't see the look on her face.

"You ended the school year in good shape, but, champ, you were behind before that. That means you're still going to start middle school a few steps back."

"I'll catch up, Dad, I promise." She could hear her own voice tightening like a spring. "I'll study, like, ten hours a day when school starts again."

Dad closed his eyes and got still. She was in pointless-to-argue territory, and it made her want to crawl under the bed and start up the catfight again. It seemed to work for Lolli and Artemis when *they* were frustrated.

"Your middle school teachers are going to expect your skills to be seventh-grade level," Dad said. "Right now, Mr. Auggy says they're about mid-sixth, which is great considering what they were in January. So here's the deal."

Lucy held back a grunt. It was only a deal if both people agreed to it.

"You'll work with Mr. Auggy until you get your reading up to seventh-grade level. That could take all summer, or it could take a couple of weeks. That's up to you."

Lucy looked at him sharply. "What if I get it there in three days?"

"Then you're done. We'll check it periodically, of course, to make sure it stays there."

"It will," Lucy said. But she hoped her outside voice sounded more sure than the one screaming inside her brain: *What are you thinking, Lucy? You can't do this!*

The world didn't have enough exclamation points to end that sentence.

"Okay," Dad said as he stood up and got his shifting gaze pretty close to her eyes. "That's taken care of, then."

It was his way of saying they wouldn't be discussing this any more. Which left only one thing to do. As soon as Lucy heard Dad outside saying, "Morning, Luke," she looked through the window to watch as he climbed into the passenger's seat of his assistant's car and took off for the radio station. Then she pushed open the screen and whistled—loud—between her teeth into the New Mexican morning. J.J. wouldn't think that was a very cool signal, but it was the best she could do in an emergency—especially since he was probably still asleep. Without waiting for an answer from J.J.'s falling-down house across the street, she scribbled on a piece of paper:

Inez,

I went to the soccer field with J.J. I'll be back by lunch.
Can we have your tamales? They're my favorite.

Lucy

Lucy propped the note on the kitchen table between the sombrero-shaped salt and pepper shakers. Inez might be a little peeved that Lucy left before she came, but the part about loving her tamales would soften her up.

She slung her soccer ball bag over her shoulder, and by the time she got to her bike, which was leaning against the Mexican elder tree in the backyard, Mudge was already growling outside the gate. That meant J.J. was there waiting. He never dared try to get past their curmudgeon he-cat. He wasn't crazy about any cats, but especially not Mudge.

Lucy rubbed the top of Mudge's tabby head with her foot as she rolled her bike out. J.J. was already straddling his bike, his Apache-black hair smashed under his backward ball cap and into its usual ponytail at the base of his neck. The wrinkles of his pillowcase were still carved into the side of his face.

"What's up?" he said.

"Evil," Lucy said.

"Aunt Karen?"

"Unh-uh. My dad."

He gave her a long look as he pedaled to keep up with her.

"Yeah, go figure," Lucy said.

"Your dad's cool."

"Not today." Lucy made a sharp turn onto Granada Street, away from the Sacramento Mountains that loomed behind them like protective uncles. "I have to do *school* this summer," she barked over her shoulder.

"No way."

"Way."

J.J. pulled up beside her, his blue eyes narrowed like a hawk's. "I'd run away."

That was J.J.'s automatic answer to every parent problem, and he had plenty of them. Lucy shook her head.

"What are you gonna do?" he said.

"Oh, I'm gonna do it. I have to. But I don't have to like it."

"Wanna play soccer?"

"Have we met? Yes, I wanna play soccer."

They pulled up to the edge of Highway 54, and Lucy squinted a grin into the sun. She and J.J. and their soccer field. With that combination, maybe this day could be fixed. .

The air was still crisp and woven with sunlight as J.J. led the way across the highway and then the bridge over the trickle-like irrigation ditch. Lucy heard a distant rumble of thunder, but she ignored it. The sky was so big in southern New Mexico, you could hear thunder and see lightning from what seemed like a bajillion miles away, even over the tops of the bare-faced mountains that surrounded them on all sides. Rain was a different story. She and Dad didn't even own an umbrella.

Besides, if a few drops fell, that wouldn't stop her and J.J. and their soccer game. Lucy's grin widened as they rounded the bend in the dirt road and zipped under the red-white-and-blue sign Veronica and Dusty's moms had painted: "Los Suenos Soccer Field, Home of the Los Suenos Dreams." Lucy had her bike behind the bleachers and the ball out of the bag almost before J.J. was off his seat.

"One-on-One!" she called out. "Bet you can't score on me, J.J.!"

"Bet you can't stop me!"

They used the penalty mark as one goal and the real goal area as the other and turned and faked themselves dizzy. Neither of them scored—until Lucy did a perfect shimmy to one side and kicked the ball in the other direction, right past J.J. and over the line.

She threw her head back to cheer into the sky and froze with her mouth open. Somewhere between the turning and the faking, clouds blacker than Lollipop the kitty had formed, and even as Lucy stared, one of them spit out a mouthful of lightning that crackled through the power line above the refreshment building. The thunder smacked into Lucy's ears and rooted her to the ground.

"Come on!" J.J. yelled, and he grabbed her sleeve and hauled her out of the goal area. Before they could get to their bikes, the sky flashed again and then again, and the thunder was so loud Lucy couldn't hear what else J.J. was yelling. She dove for her handlebars, but he pushed her under the bleachers, just as a torrent of rain beat down on them with drops sharp as needles.

"Holy frijoles!" Lucy said.

J.J. turned his backward cap around, but even under the bleacher seats, water slid down the bill and plastered his shorts to his legs. Lucy shook her head to get the rain out of her eyes and smacked J.J. in the cheek with her ponytail. He didn't even flinch.

"I didn't see that coming!" Lucy said. "Guess we oughta just wait it out, huh?"

J.J. hunched his shoulders and peered out at the rain that now came down in sheets. "Guess so," he said.

But ten minutes later, as a lake formed between them and the fence and the storm battered on, J.J. shook his head. "Better make a run for it," he said.

Lucy tried, but the wind and the slapping rain pushed her back a step for every two she took forward.

"Leave the bikes—we'll get 'em later!" J.J. shouted.

He hooked his arm through Lucy's and pulled her around the giant puddle that was by now taking up most of the area behind the bleachers. They sloshed through another one that had formed outside the fence, and Lucy had to tuck her chin to keep the rain from shooting its bullets into her eyes. When J.J. stopped, she peeked over his shoulder and nearly bit into it.

The dirt road was a river, charging past them as if it had someplace important to go. Even as they stood there, the water raced over Lucy's toes and pulled at her feet.

"Hold on!" J.J. yelled.

Lucy wrapped her arms around J.J.'s, one hand clinging like a monkey to his T-shirt, as he picked his way along the mini-river that widened by the minute. Plastic bottles and crushed-up cans tumbled past, and Lucy tried not to imagine herself and J.J. falling in and hurtling with them to who-knew-where. She placed her feet exactly where J.J. had put his, but even at that, she slid in the mud and went down on her knees. The water tried to drag her with it.

J.J. stopped and stooped over. "Get on my back!"

"You can't carry me!" Lucy shouted—though she was sure the next crash of thunder stole her words.

"Get on!" J.J. said.

Lucy did and braced her arms around his neck as he half-ran, half-slid to the bridge. The trickle of water from the irrigation ditch had now swollen over the banks and ripped at the underside of the bridge as J.J. careened across with Lucy hanging on. The ground was higher on that side, and the water only covered their ankles. Lucy slid off of J.J.'s back just as the air cracked again. Only this time, it wasn't thunder.

She gazed in horror as the bridge collapsed behind them.

2

The bridge caved into a *V*, and Lucy felt her knees cave too.

"Come on!" J.J. cried out.

She could barely hear him over the crashing of planks and the angry protests of the water below. Somehow she was able to run after him, sloshing through the rising water to the highway. Ahead of them, Sheriff Navarro's cruiser blocked the intersection, and the sheriff himself stood in thigh-high boots in the middle of it, waving off the few cars that tried to crawl through like turtles going uphill.

J.J.'s ponytail flapped from side to side, and Lucy knew he was looking for a way to escape before the sheriff saw them. Lucy grabbed his arm and pulled him toward the car. By now, its hubcaps had all but disappeared into the Highway 54 river.

Sheriff Navarro peered at them from under the dripping bill of his hat, and even through the downpour, Lucy could see the I-should-have-known-it-was-you-two in his sharp, black eyes. She'd seen that look plenty of times, from the sheriff *and* his son.

"Get in the car!" was all he said.

Lucy kept a tight grip on J.J.'s T-shirt so he wouldn't bolt and waded with him to the cruiser. The sheriff could barely get the door open to let them in. They were already soaking the backseat when he climbed into the front.

"I'm not even gonna ask what you're doing out in this," he said.

That was good, because J.J. probably wasn't going to answer, which meant Lucy would have to think of something, and right now all she wanted to do was get home to Dad.

"I gotta park this thing anyway before it turns into a boat," the sheriff said, more to himself than to them. He didn't talk to kids that much.

Then he didn't say anything at all as the car nearly floated down Granada Street and fishtailed to a stop in front of Lucy's house. He twisted to look over the seat.

"I'm gonna have to carry you kids in."

J.J. just grunted and opened the door. Water rushed onto the floorboards and drowned his feet, but J.J. splashed out and flailed his way across the now-flooded street toward his house. His front yard was a sea of broken bicycles and wash tubs and old tires, all bobbing like bathtub toys. Lucy hoped he didn't get bonked in the head with any of it as he swam for his front door.

"Let's go," Sheriff Navarro said to her, and he didn't wait for Lucy to climb onto his back. He just hauled her out of the car and threw her over his shoulder the way she'd seen firemen rescue people from burning buildings on TV. She sure hoped none of her friends were witnessing this.

But Mora was at the kitchen window, of course, her always-huge brown eyes twice their normal size as she watched Lucy pass by practically upside down. Lucy could see that Mora's lips were fully operational. She was probably giving Inez an inch-by-inch description of Lucy being delivered like a sandbag to the back porch.

Inez met them, barely able to keep the door from blowing off as Sheriff Navarro deposited Lucy inside.

"Don't let her out," he shouted at Inez above the wind. "We got flash flooding. I'm surprised she didn't drown already."

"*Gracias,* Senor Sheriff," Inez said. "You want to come in and dry your—"

Sheriff Navarro just grunted at her and, to Lucy's relief, ducked back into the storm. It was going to be bad enough enduring what Inez had to say. She didn't need both of them telling her she should know enough to come in out of the rain. She would rather hear it from Inez anyway. It wasn't so bad in Spanish.

"Oh, my gosh, you're, like, totally soaked!" Mora said from her perch on the edge of the kitchen sink. Her fingers, as usual, were punctuating every word in the air. She was all about exclamation points, too.

"Seriously?" Lucy said.

Inez grunted. "Mora, get the towels for Senorita Lucy."

"Towels? She needs, like, a giant blow-dryer."

But Mora didn't have to be asked twice. You didn't argue with Inez, even though her English wasn't that good. She was a short lady with a haircut like a little Dutch boy, only black instead of blond, but she had powerful eyes and a voice that got bigger the more softly she talked.

Mora produced five towels, and Inez rubbed at Lucy until her skin was almost raw, all the while muttering things in Spanish. Even if Lucy could have understood what she was saying, she couldn't have heard it over Mora's babbling.

"We totally thought you drowned. We tried to call your dad, only the phone is out. I almost freaked, and *Abuela* was, like, 'The Lord, he will take care of Senorita Lucy,' and she's all praying, and I'm thinking, 'Well, if she drowns, at least she's with J.J. — "

Lucy was glad to be sent off to the shower by Inez. Mora could talk longer than you could listen to her sometimes, and about the weirdest things.

When Lucy came out in dry clothes, Inez had tortilla soup and hot tea ready. Lucy put Marmalade, their orange kitty, in her lap and drank her tea out of the butterfly mug that had been her mom's. Mora sat across from her, cross-legged in the chair, and picked up where she'd left off.

"Okay, so, like, how deep is it out there? Could you swim in it? I would have been so freaked out — "

Lucy clapped her hand over Mora's still-moving mouth and leaned into the radio on the table. Dad's voice crackled from it.

"The National Weather Service is reporting — " Big pause. " — frontal winds of thirty miles per hour." Another pause. "Make that fifty. Gusts up to fifty."

Lucy felt a frown form. Dad was usually so smooth on the radio.

Listening to him was like hearing molasses pour, people said. Lucy had never actually heard molasses pour, but she knew what they meant. He never said "um" or "uh" or "like," which Mora would have said every other word if she were a radio announcer. But today he sounded more like a car engine that couldn't quite start.

"Because of our sparse vegetation here in New Mexico," Dad said, "the runoffs from this storm can cause flash flooding."

"Ya think?" Mora said to the radio. "No offense, Mr. Rooney, but that already happened."

Lucy was glad Dad couldn't hear her. She glared at Mora and turned up the volume.

"Today is a good day to stay home," Dad was saying. "We'll keep you updated, so just sit back with a cup of coffee and count on us. We'll ..."

Another big pause. Lucy turned up the volume again, but there was only silence.

"What happened to him?" she said.

"Senor Ted, he is fine," Inez said. "The radio, it is not." She nodded at the light over the table that flickered and blinked into darkness.

"The power's off?" Mora wailed. "I wanted to watch *The View.*"

Lucy didn't know what that was, and she didn't care. She had a sudden icky-achy feeling in her stomach.

"You think my dad's okay, Inez?" she said.

"Senor Ted, he can take care of Senor Ted." Inez poured more tea into Lucy's cup. "And I can take care of you."

But as Lucy watched the wind slam the rain against the window, she felt a scared kind of lonely. Dad always said that once you've lost somebody you loved, it was hard to trust that it wouldn't happen again. That was why they had God.

God and soccer. There were drills she could do in the house if she moved the furniture around some. She could at least toss the ball into the air and catch it with her foot. Lucy pushed the tea mug aside and went for the hook by the back door where she kept her ball in its net bag. She was halfway there when she realized she'd left it on the soccer field. Now she *was* ready to freak.

"What's wrong?" Mora said. "You look all weirded out."

"My soccer ball's probably floated all the way to Alamogordo by now," Lucy said. "Not to mention my bike."

She stuck her hands in her pockets, pulled them out, picked up Marmalade, put him down. Her skin itched on the inside. And then she realized something else.

"Oh, my gosh!" she said. "Where's Mudge? He's out in this!"

She tore for the door, but Inez got between her and it.

"He's in the house," Mora said. "Abuela has the scratches to prove it."

"He is under Senor Ted's bed. Come. Sit." Inez pointed to the table. "We will talk."

"About what?" Mora said. Her eyes were already in suspicious slits.

"Senorita Esther."

"Who?"

Inez reached into her bag on the counter and pulled out a beat-up looking leather book.

"Bible study?" Mora said. "Abuela—it's summer!" An exclamation point came out of her finger. "Why do we have to 'study' in the summer?"

She didn't even know the half of it. Lucy sank into a kitchen chair. It seemed like a long time ago that Dad told her she had to do school-work all summer. She wished he was here saying it now. She would listen to it a hundred times.

Inez waited until Mora had flopped into a chair before she turned the thin-as-onionskin pages and folded her hands on them.

"This is the story of Senorita Hadassah," she said.

"I thought you said her name was Ethel," Mora said.

"Esther," Lucy said.

Inez shook her head. "Her name when she is born is Hadassah. People now call her Esther. It is word for 'the star.'"

Mora gave a dramatic sigh. "I wish I could change my name. I want to be 'Madeline.' Don't I look like a Madeline to you?"

"Poor Senorita Esther," Inez said, ignoring her. "Her parents, they have die, and she lives with her cousin Senor Mordecai."

"Now there's a name I would definitely change," Mora said.

Lucy leaned into the table. "What happened to her parents?"

"The Bible, it does not tell us," Inez said.

Lucy nodded. She was relating to this Esther person already. Mora, on the other hand, was twirling a strand of her coffee-colored hair around her finger and looking like she'd rather be taking a math test.

"Is her cousin nice to her?" Lucy said.

"Sí. He is good to Senorita Esther and tells her she will have a fine husband and children someday."

Mora showed a flicker of interest. "So he lets her date. I'm down with that."

"And then one day," Inez said.

Mora rolled her eyes. "I knew it was too good to be true. What happened?"

"King Xerxes, he send his men into the neighborhood."

"Where did they get these *names?*" Mora said.

"They are looking for a new queen for the king and want to see all the beautiful young girls."

"What happened to the old queen?" Lucy said.

"She probably got fat or something, and he wanted a younger model." Mora's eyes rolled again. "Men are so fickle."

"The queen, she disobeys the king," Inez said. "He sends her away. He will have a new queen who will show him the respect."

"So why can't he find his own woman?" Mora said. "Is he ugly or something?"

Lucy groaned. "For Pete's sake, Mora—let her tell the story."

"They will bring to him every beautiful young girl," Inez said. "The senoritas, they will have the beauty treatments for six months, and then he will choose."

Mora's big brown eyes went dreamy. "I would definitely want a chance at that. It would be like *American Idol.* Even if you didn't win, you'd be famous and some other guy would marry you—like a prince or somebody."

Inez was shaking her head. "The girls he does not choose will stay in the palace forever."

"What?" Mora's hands sprung out like springs. "That is just wrong! I just wouldn't go, then."

"Senorita Esther, she does not have the choice. She must leave her cousin and her friends and do what the king says."

Lucy thought Mora was going to jump over the table. She had to admit it sounded like a pretty bad deal. As much as Mora got on her nerves, if she had to leave, Lucy would miss her. And if Dad had to go —

"There is one more thing that is *muy difícil* for Senorita Esther," Inez said.

Mora looked at Lucy. "That means 'way hard.'"

"I got that," Lucy said.

"Esther, she is a Jew, and the king, he is not. If he will discover this about her, he may be very angry." Inez leaned in as if she were about to tell a secret. "Senor Mordecai, he says Senorita Esther must never tell at the palace that she is a Jew."

Mora shrugged. "What's so hard about that?"

Lucy didn't answer, but she thought she knew. It would be like not being able to talk about God to anybody, just when God was starting to make sense to her. What if she couldn't keep her Book of Lists where she talked to God?

She'd probably start throwing soccer balls at people.

"Okay, so, does she go through the beauty treatments or what?" Mora circled her hand for Inez to get on with the story. "It might be worth it if you came out looking like a model or something."

Lucy definitely didn't agree with that as Inez read about Esther's beauty coach soaking her skin in oil of myrrh and her hair in cinnamon perfume. It sounded more like marinating a chicken than getting ready for some king she might not even like anyway.

Lucy was about to check out on this story and dream up some soccer strategies instead when Inez said, "Senor Mordecai, he knows that Senorita Esther, she is sick for her home. And so every day, he comes to the court to visit her."

"Are you serious?" Mora said. "I wouldn't be homesick. I would be totally loving it there!"

Lucy decided she would not be "loving it" at all. It sounded way too much like Aunt Karen coming in to do a makeover on her. She tucked her feet up under her and wished they could heat more water for tea and that the radio would come back on so she could at least hear Dad and know he was okay.

"All right," Mora said, hands on skinny hips, "so does she get picked for queen or not?"

Inez closed the Bible and folded her hands neatly on top of it. "Next time," she said.

"Hello! I'm dying here!" Mora said.

"You will not die, Mora," Inez assured her.

Mora probably would have argued that, but a pounding on the back door lifted all three of them from their chairs and sent Marmalade skittering to try to squeeze behind the stove. With fear batting at her stomach, Lucy got to the door first and saw Mr. Auggy's wet face smiling its small smile through the glass.

Inez had the towels ready before Lucy got the door open, but Mr. Auggy held onto the door frame like he was trying to keep from blowing away.

"Can't stay!" he said. "I have a message from your dad."

Lucy took a step forward, but Inez held her by the back of her T-shirt.

"He says to tell you he's fine, but he's stuck at the station. Can Inez stay with you?"

"Sí, sí, sí," Inez said behind Lucy.

"Can you take me to my dad in your Jeep?" Lucy said.

Mr. Auggy's small smile reappeared. "Even my Jeep won't make it out here. I'm in my kayak."

Lucy noticed for the first time that he was wearing a life jacket. That wasn't something you saw too often in the desert. It was all way too scary.

"It'll be all right, captain," Mr. Auggy shouted over the wind. "You hold down the fort here, and your dad'll be back as soon as he can."

Why can't you bring him home in your kayak? Lucy wanted to say. *I need my Dad.*

24

But Mr. Auggy slogged off the side of the porch without hearing the exclamation points in her head.

3

Dear God: Why This Is the Longest Night Ever

1. Because Mora is talking in her sleep. Nonstop. Just like when she's awake, only she isn't making any sense. Which isn't really all that different from when she's awake.
2. Because there's no place for my dad to sleep at the radio station except on that lumpy couch that has springs that poke you in the behind if you sit wrong.
3. Because —

"Ow!"

Lucy reached behind her and swatted at Lollipop with her flashlight. The kitty's claws stuck to Lucy's T-shirt, and she protested at being shaken off. Mora just kept muttering in her dreams.

Lolli keeps jumping on me, and Artemis Hamm is growling under the bed, and Marmalade is pacing all around looking for Dad. The only cat who's quiet is Mudge. He's on top of the refrigerator.

Lucy shined her light on the Book of Lists again and chewed on the end of her pen. None of it would be so bad except for the fourth reason, and she didn't want to write it down because then it would be real.

Du-uh. She was telling it to God, so it was real already.

4. Because I'm scared Dad will never come home like Mom didn't come home from Iraq. The radio station might blow up like her hotel did — or it'll sink into the mud or something. Then I won't have a mom OR a dad.

Lucy shivered and was about to let the tears come that she'd been holding back ever since Mr. Auggy was there, when a light flickered across her bedroom wall.

A J.J. light.

Lucy scrambled to the window and cupped her hands around her eyes. The rain had finally stopped, but the night was inky-black without the streetlights. That made it perfect for the big Maglite J.J. was swishing around into the darkness outside his room. Lucy dug her own flashlight out from under her mattress and flicked it on and then off and then on again. J.J. answered with a figure eight and seven circles. She didn't know what that meant, but just having J.J. in his window was enough to make it better.

She was about to sink back to her bed when J.J. shined the light right into his own face so Lucy could see his mouth. He moved it slow and big like it was a piece of rubber. She was pretty sure it said, "Soccer tomorrow."

Okay, so it was *definitely* better. She finally fell asleep hugging her flashlight and her Book of Lists and listening to Mora dream of beauty treatments.

Mora was still mumbling in her sleep when Lucy opened her eyes, but she knew at once that it was the tapping of pebbles on her window that had woken her up. She didn't even have to look out to know that J.J. was hanging out at his front fence with a handful of stones and a half-grin.

But she got to her knees and peered through the window. She was correct, of course. He was standing on top of a pile of old tires stacked against the fence, jiggling pebbles in his hand.

'I'll be right out,' she motioned to him.

She hopped out of bed and over Mora and into shorts and a t-shirt. Nobody stirred, not even a kitty or Inez. Still no sign of Dad.

The sun was shining, but the world did not look cheerful when Lucy met J.J. outside her gate. The streets were caked in mud and strewn with cottonwood limbs, and most of the lighter junk from J.J.'s front yard—rags and bicycle wheels and battered hubcaps—was hanging on his caved-in fence. A telephone company truck had already pulled up to a pole across the street, and Mr. Benitez, the grocery store owner, was stabbing his finger at the worker who climbed it.

"Look, we'll get it done as fast as we can," the man called down. "The storm took out all the lines in town."

"I've got a business to run!" Mr. Benitez snapped at him.

"Join the club," the man snapped back.

"Let's get outta here," J.J. grunted to Lucy under his breath.

"Yeah, seriously." Mr. Benitez wasn't all that nice when he was in a *good* mood. This probably wasn't going to end well.

"I just have to go tell Inez where we're going," Lucy said. "I'll be right back."

If she couldn't hear from Dad for a while, she'd better stay busy. Another hour in the house with Mora didn't qualify as "busy." It qualified as "nuts." Besides, maybe she and J.J. could go to Dad themselves...

Lucy had a note composed in her head when she slipped back into the kitchen, but Inez was up, slicing into bread with a knife and into Lucy with her gaze. She didn't even have any of the crusty sleep-things in her eyes that Lucy was still picking out of hers.

"It's okay if I go check things out with J.J., right?" Lucy said.

"What things are these?" Inez bent her head over the loaf, but Lucy knew she was seeing right into her brain.

"The soccer field?" Lucy said.

"This is a question?" Inez said,

"The soccer field. We want to see what happened to it,"

"Only there."

Lucy felt herself sag. "Maybe we'll also go—"

"Maybe you will also come home after."

Inez looked up, and her eyes got soft. "Senor Ted will come home," she said.

How Inez knew she *was* planning to go out to the radio station *if* she found her bike, Lucy didn't know. But somehow Inez did, and that was the end of it. With a glower at the top of Inez's head as she went back to the bread, Lucy sighed her way out the back door. By the gate, J.J. was doing some glowering of his own, at his little sister Januarie who had joined him. But then, he was always glowering at her.

"I'm going with you," Januarie announced. She had the kind of voice a Chihuahua would have if it could talk.

"No, you're not," J.J. said.

Januarie's eyes narrowed in her round face, fringed in dark hair that wouldn't stay in its ponytails. "Who's going to stop me?"

J.J. looked at Lucy, who shrugged. Now that Januarie was nine, she was more annoying than she'd been at eight, but they couldn't ditch her. With her and J.J.'s dad not allowed to see them because he was so mean to J.J., and their mom "not handling it well," as Dad put it, everybody in town had to watch over Januarie. If either she or J.J. got into any trouble at all—like if J.J. got into a fight the way his dad always did—that would mean their mom couldn't control them, and then Winnie the State Lady would come and put them in foster care. Lucy was pretty sure that wasn't going to happen, because J.J. would rather put up with Januarie than be like his father.

"You have to keep up on your own then," J.J. said to Januarie as he strode off down Granada Street. "We're not waitin' for ya."

Januarie's chubby legs went into gear beside Lucy, and she was quiet until they got to Pasco's Café.

"I'm hungry," she said.

"Didn't you have any breakfast?" Lucy said.

"Like that ever made a difference." J.J. clamped his jaw down. He was done talking, Lucy knew.

They stopped at Highway 54, and Januarie pulled the back of her hand across her sweaty forehead. "It's hot. I wish we could ride our bikes."

"I hope I even have a bike now," Lucy said. If she did, she would be walking it home anyway. All the streets were layered in mud, and the broken branches had turned them into an obstacle course. They couldn't have gone all the way out to Dad's station even if Inez had let her. How was he supposed to get home?

And for that matter ... Lucy stopped when they got to the other side of the highway. "How are we gonna get across the ditch?" she said. "The bridge is out, remember?"

"Jump," J.J. said.

"What if I fall in?" Januarie said.

Lucy put her hand up. "Don't answer that, J.J."

As it turned out, the irrigation ditch had already shrunk to a trickle and a half, and it dug confused new paths around the hunks of fallen wood. They used them for stepping stones, though Januarie couldn't seem to keep her feet out of the mud. She was trailing heavily behind them, wailing out complaints, as they rounded the bend to the soccer field. Once J.J. and Lucy were there, though, Januarie had no trouble catching up with them, because they could only stand and stare.

Their sign, so bright and proud the day before, was on its face in the mud, poles snapped in half. The bleachers were in splinters, scattered across their beloved field ... or what was left of it. The center was crisscrossed in eroded rivulets. The sides had completely washed against the fence on one side and into the slivered bleachers on the other. Neither Lucy's soccer ball nor her bike or J.J.'s was anywhere to be seen.

But the worst was the refreshment stand, which teetered at a slant like a dizzy old man. The roof was scattered in shards on the field and along the fence. Lucy imagined a giant school-yard bully, stomping through and tearing it all apart, just for spite.

"Oh—my—gosh!!!!!!"

Lucy didn't have to turn around to know that Veronica had arrived, and she felt Dusty beside her, pawing for her hand with her own hot-chocolate-colored one.

"This is horrible," Dusty said. Her usually creamy heart-shaped face was as pale as Inez's porridge, and her golden-brown eyes were open so wide Lucy was sure she'd never get them closed again.

'Horrible' didn't even begin to describe it, as far as Lucy was concerned, but she didn't know what word did. Nobody else even tried to find one. When Oscar and Emanuel got there, they gnawed on their toothpicks and looked at Lucy like they always did when there was a decision to be made. But she didn't know where to start.

Veronica's mouth hung partway down, a sure sign she couldn't wrap her mind around what was going on. One dark finger twirled a hunk of her thick fudge-colored hair.. "If Carla Rosa were here, she'd say, 'Guess what? It's ruined.'"

"It is," J.J. said.

"Well, now, wait a minute." Dusty squeezed Lucy's hand tighter. "It could probably be fixed, right, *Bolillo?*"

The nickname that always made Lucy smile didn't do the trick this time.

"Couldn't it?" Veronica said, furrowing her forehead into caramel rows. "Our moms would paint a new sign."

"Yeah." Oscar looked up at skinny, bony Emanuel and poked him with a square fist for no apparent reason. "Gabe's old man always has convicts that needs to work. They could fix them bleachers like they done before."

Lucy didn't say anything. Sheriff Navarro didn't have "convicts." He had people that needed to work off speeding tickets and stuff, but there weren't enough lawbreakers in all of Tularosa County to rebuild those bleachers. They'd have to start over—and she was pretty sure it wasn't going to happen before their game in two weeks.

Emanuel lifted a lanky arm and pointed toward the gate. As if he'd heard them talking about him, the sheriff pulled up in his cruiser. Through the windshield, Lucy could see his brows hooding his eyes the way they did when he was *really* unhappy. J.J. edged away.

As Sheriff Navarro climbed out of the car and picked his way through the mud toward them, Lucy kind of wanted to slip off, too, though not for the same reason as J.J. Even though the sheriff said he was on J.J.'s side and didn't want him to have to leave his house and his mom, J.J. didn't seem to believe that anymore than he believed in the Easter Bunny. It seemed like he was just waiting for the day when Sheriff Navarro would drag him off to foster care just for breathing wrong or something. Lucy's not wanting to be around the guy was way different. About half the time he said stuff that made *her* want to say stuff that Dad didn't want her saying to grown-ups—and now was probably one of those times.

"Gabe said I'd find you all here," the sheriff said when he reached them. "He wanted to come, but I didn't let him."

Lucy actually felt a little bad about that. Gabe could be a creature from Rudesville sometimes—but he was part of the team, and he needed to see this.

"Sorry about your field," Sheriff Navarro said.

Lucy studied him. Okay, his mouth did kind of droop at the corners, and the spray of sun-squinty lines around his eyes looked more sad than mad. But he still had that what-are-you-kids-trying-to-get-away-with edge in his voice. Sheriffs must learn that in police school, she thought.

"I know you're proud of it," he said. "Whole town's proud of it."

"We can fix it, can't we?" Dusty pulled Lucy and Veronica close to her. "We'll all help."

The sheriff pulled his hand across his eyes, and Lucy noticed that it looked like they had backpacks under them. He must have been up late.

"I don't know," he said. "That's up to the town council, and right now, we've got a few other things to worry about." He narrowed his very-black eyes at the bleachers and then at what used to be the refreshment building. "This place sure took it heavier than anything else in town."

"Figures," J.J. said under his breath.

"Well, for now, you all need to clear out." The sheriff waved toward the gate. "It's not safe here until we can assess the damage."

"What does 'assess' mean?" Lucy said.

"It means we have to figure out how bad it is."

Lucy held back a grunt. She could tell them *that*. It was destroyed.

They had to start from the beginning again, and Lucy wanted to do it right now.

But it was clear that Sheriff Navarro wasn't letting any of them out of his sight. Lucy looked around again for her bike — and spied a twisted piece of metal stuck under one of the fallen bleacher seats. It might as well have been a scrap in J.J.'s yard. This was turning out to be the most *un*perfect summer ever.

Lucy could feel Sheriff Navarro watching the seven of them as they straggled away from the tumbled bleachers, but when Lucy looked back, he had shifted his focus to the leaning refreshment stand. Arms bowed out at his sides, he approached it like the cops did on TV when they were onto something.

"What, Lucy?" Dusty whispered, hugging Lucy's arm.

"We should go," Veronica said. "My mom doesn't even know I'm here. If the sheriff brings me home, I am in so much trouble."

"Busted," Oscar said, though without his usual wicked smile.

"I'm coming," Lucy said, but she stayed a few seconds longer. Sheriff Navarro squatted beside the refreshment stand and peered closely at the mud. He wasn't looking at wind damage, that was for sure.

"I'm hungry!" Januarie wailed.

Lucy didn't see how she could even think about food. Her stomach was one giant knot. She stepped over a tangle of splintered wood and went to what was left of her bike. It was bent beyond hope, even though it was still hanging together — except for one hunk of metal that lay a few feet away.

But when Lucy leaned over to pick it up, she realized it didn't belong to her bike at all. It was heavy and straight and looked like some kind of tool. She looked around to see where it might have come from, and her eyes snagged right on J.J. who had come up behind her. He was staring at it as if he knew it from someplace.

"What is this thing?" she said to him under her breath.

He glanced back at the others, who were almost to the road now.

"Tire iron," he said.

"Somebody was changing a tire out here? Nah — it had to blow from someplace." Lucy felt her eyes bulge. "That wind was stronger than I thought."

"No, it wasn't," J.J. said. And from the way he clamped down his jaw, Lucy knew that was *all* he was going to say. Something dark passed through her. Something she couldn't even name.

Things did brighten up a little when she got home and saw that Inez's truck was gone, which meant a Mora-break, And—even better—she could see Dad and Mr. Auggy through the kitchen window. Lucy took the back steps two at a time, but she stopped at the door when she heard Mr. Auggy's voice. He was using the serious tone she didn't hear that much from him.

"I'm with you, Ted," Mr. Auggy said. "I didn't see any other property in town torn up like it was. I didn't get *that* close a look at it because it was still dark, but at first pass—I'm thinking something more than the storm hit it."

"Really?" Dad said.

"Maybe I'm just overreacting."

Overreacting to what? Were they talking about what she *thought* they were talking about?

Lucy shoved open the door, and the smiles appeared that meant a change of subject because a kid was there. Besides, Dad had his arms open, and Lucy had to fly into them.

"Are you okay?" she said as she dove against his chest.

"I had an adventure, that's all." Dad chuckled. "The good thing is, it didn't make any difference to me that the lights were out. You survived okay?"

"Yeah, me and Mora didn't hurt each other, so I guess that's good." Lucy looked at Mr. Auggy through the crook in Dad's arm. "Mora and *I*."

"See that?" Dad said. "She's improving already."

Lucy almost groaned. She'd hoped with the storm, he might have forgotten about the whole tutoring thing. Fat chance, evidently.

"So you and I are going to be working on *all* your skills this summer, captain," Mr. Auggy said. "Not just soccer."

Lucy sank into a chair and rolled up the edge of the tablecloth. "I don't see how we're gonna work on my soccer skills without a field."

Mr. Auggy smiled his small smile. "Oh, ye of little faith."

"What does that mean?" Lucy said.

"It means I have a plan, if you and your dad can work it out."

"What plan?" Why could grown-ups never just get to the point?

"I've been asked to work at a youth soccer camp in Las Cruces," Mr. Auggy said. "It's a day camp, lasts three weeks, and even though it's a little late, they have some spaces left for the Dreams."

"You mean, our whole team?"

"Anybody who can get the money together by Monday."

Before Lucy's heart could sink too far, Mr. Auggy put his hand up. "Don't worry about J.J. and Januarie. I can bring two players for free because I'm going to be on staff. I'm pretty sure everyone else will be okay—it isn't that expensive."

Lucy looked at Dad, but he was already nodding.

"Are you *serious?*" Lucy said.

"As a heart attack," Mr. Auggy said, "And here's the best part for you, captain."

Lucy didn't see how it could get any better, but she bobbed her head anyway.

"This is a top soccer camp, which means scouts from the Olympic Development Team will be there to watch the final games. If they like a player, they'll invite her to participate in the regional tryouts, without even having to apply."

A thrill charged straight through Lucy.

Mr. Auggy stood and passed a hand over Dad's shoulder. "I'm going to leave you two to work the rest of it out."

Dad went to the door with him and they stepped out onto the back porch. Lucy was pretty sure they were picking up where they'd left off when she got home, and she was tempted to tiptoe over and eavesdrop. But Dad could practically hear a flea springing off one of the cats, and he had special radar for her, so she stayed at the table and let Marmalade curl up in her lap.

Was she really going to get to go to soccer camp, she thought as she stroked his orange back. And have a chance at ODP even sooner than she thought? It sounded like it—and yet there was whatever Mr. Auggy said she and Dad had to 'work out.' That never ended up being a good deal. The last thing they'd 'worked out' was her having to do schoolwork over the summer.

Dad came back to the table, but she couldn't read his face, so she went right in.

"What 'rest of it'?" she asked. "Dad—I totally want to do this."

"Just one small piece," he said. He sat down again across from her, and Marmalade jumped back to his lap, which he much preferred over anybody's.

"I can already tell it's not that small," Lucy said.

"That's up to you. I think this soccer camp will be a great opportunity for you, Luce—"

"What's the but?"

"No but, just a because. It's going to be good for you because it'll teach you how to handle both your sport and your schoolwork the way you're going to have to do next year in seventh grade."

Sure sounded like a 'but' to Lucy.

"You can stay in soccer camp," Dad said, "as long as you make weekly progress with your reading skills. Fair enough?"

His eyes settled on her. It was one of those times she just knew he could see her. She wrestled a smile to her face.

"Is that all?" she said. "I thought you were going to ask me to do something *hard*."

"That's my Champ," Dad said.

But Lucy didn't feel like much of a champ as she skipped a kiss over the top of his head and went back out to look for J.J. Maybe she'd convinced Dad, and maybe Marmalade, that she thought this was going to be a piece of cake. But she sure hadn't convinced herself

4

Why I Think You (God) Might Be Making This
Summer Perfect After All

1. Everybody on the team gets to go to soccer camp.
2. Even Oscar, because after we found out his mom didn't
   have the money and he doesn't have an "old man"
   like he always says, Dusty had a pool party for her
   birthday and asked everybody to bring money for Oscar
   instead of presents for her.
3. Mr. Auggy said we were good Christians for doing that
   for Oscar, but it was all Dusty's idea. She's so good, I
   feel like a jerk next to her sometimes.
4. Dusty and Veronica and Emanuel and Carla Rosa's moms
   are taking turns driving us to camp. It'll take two vehicles
   to get all of us in plus our cleats and shin guards and
   water bottles and towels and stuff.

Lucy scratched behind Lolli's left ear with her pen. She was feeling
so perfect, and then that missing-Mom twinge happened in her throat.
Her mom would have been the best soccer-mom ever. She'd have juice
boxes for everybody, even though they all had their own water, and
she wouldn't make them listen to elevator music in the car, and she
would know good questions to ask about soccer—not just, "So how
was it? Did you have fun?"

Lucy swallowed the twinge and went back to the Book of Lists.
Since it had been her mom's, it was the closest Lucy was going to get

to her. It wasn't like sitting up front with her in their own van, but it was better than nothing.

5.   Felix Pasco gave a party for the whole team at the café Saturday night. It was kind of weird because Felix had tears in his eyes when he wished us good luck and gave us all new T-shirts with Los Suenos Dreams on the back. It's always sort of scary when grown-ups look like they're going to cry.

There wasn't time to try to figure out more than that now because she could hear J.J. and Januarie arguing as they crossed the street to her gate where they were supposed to meet this morning to be picked up.

"No fighting with Artemis today," Lucy said to Lollipop over her shoulder as she rode the yellow Navajo rug down the hall to the kitchen.

"I don't fight with Artemis," Mora called sleepily from the living room where she'd dropped the minute she and Inez arrived. "I don't even know which one that is."

Lucy didn't remind Mora that not everything was about her. She had probably already gone back to sleep anyway.

Nobody on the Los Suenos team acted like they had wanted to sleep in—although Carla Rosa did say to Januarie, "Guess what? Your breath smells like you forgot to brush your teeth." Carla Rosa was always saying stuff like that, but nobody minded that much anymore because they knew she kind of couldn't help it. She and Dusty, Veronica, Januarie, and Lucy just jabbered, one voice on top of the other, all the way in Dusty's mom's SUV and howled over the signs the boys pressed to the back window of Emanuel's family minivan.

"Boys Rule; Girls Drool," one of them said.

"If Yer So Smart, How Come We're Ahead of U?" said another.

"If you're so smart, why can't you spell?" Dusty's mom said, which set the girls' group giggling. Lucy felt the twinge again. Her mom would have been funny like that too. Maybe even funnier.

But sad thoughts got left in the car when they arrived at the "ginormous" (as Veronica called it) High Noon Soccer Complex in Las Cruces, tucked into the shadows of the Organ Mountains.

"Yikes," Veronica said, lip hanging like a sofa cushion. "We're lucky to have *one* soccer field. They have one, two—"

"Four," Lucy said.

All with bleachers on both sides under roofs. And two buildings with restrooms and drinks, and a whole pavilion with picnic tables, and a grassy area with swings and stuff to climb on. There were even two rows of cottonwood trees for shade, which you didn't find much of in New Mexico. She'd never been to Disneyland, but this had to be better than that.

"This is fabulous," Dusty said to Mr. Auggy when he jogged up to them, smiling his small smile.

"Yeah, I come here all the time," Gabe said. "It's okay."

Lucy looked at J.J. If he'd been a girl, he would have rolled his eyes with her.

Mr. Auggy glanced at his watch. "Okay, I need to get you guys to your coach before the opening starts."

Lucy felt her eyes spring open. "Aren't you our coach?"

Mr. Auggy wasn't that successful with his smile this time. "No—they've asked me to work with a junior boys' team—but you'll all be together because we signed up late." He batted at the crooked ponytail on top of Januarie's head. "Except you, Jan. We're putting you with girls your own age."

She opened her mouth, and Lucy braced herself for a Chihuahua yelp. Mr. Auggy headed that off with, "You'll get to play all the time with them—nobody'll be telling you you're too little."

Actually, the Los Suenos Dreams never told her she was too little. They just told her she was bad at soccer, which made it that much better that Mr. Auggy was steering her toward a knot of giggling nine-year-olds, all with crooked ponytails.

"Sweet," J.J. said.

It was shaping up to be a *really* perfect summer for him. Lucy felt a little pang for Januarie, even though she was mostly a pain in the neck. She herself would hate to be separated from the Dreams. It was bad enough not being with Mr. Auggy, but at least they were all together.

"So—you guys the Los Suenos team?"

Lucy turned to see a taller-than-Dad guy with blackish stubble on his face that matched the fuzz on his head. He wore sunglasses that weren't all the way dark, and he only smiled with one side of his mouth.

"Oh yeah, I see it on your shirts. My bad." The guy folded his arms across his own T-shirt that said Las Cruces Soccer Camp Coach. "I'll be working with you guys."

"Guess what?" Carla Rosa said. "Some of us are girls."

Lucy thought he blinked behind the sunglasses. It was hard to tell. She looked around for Mr. Auggy, but he and Januarie were already gone.

"Yeah, well, anyway, I'm Seth. I play soccer at New Mexico State."

"Cool," Gabe said. He puffed out his chest. J.J. gave Lucy another look.

Dusty flung her arm around Lucy's shoulder. "Lucy's our captain."

"Okay, so, yeah," Seth said, "we need to get over to Field A for some kind of opening gig. I guess we're supposed to sit together so—"

He pointed in a vague direction and started walking.

"I think he wants us to follow him," Dusty whispered to Lucy.

"It would be nice if he'd tell us," she whispered back.

Veronica joined them on Lucy's other side. "Okay, he is *hot*."

Ew, Lucy thought. She was glad Mora wasn't here.

Once they got to Field A, Seth finally looked back at the team and then shaded his sunglasses with his hand as he surveyed the bleachers. All the top rows were taken, and the rest was filling up fast too. Lucy had never seen so many kids gathered in one place. Everyone was talking and moving at the same time. It all made Lucy feel small.

Seth finally herded them to the third row in the left-of-center section, right in front of a college-looking girl who was also wearing a coach T-shirt. She pulled her very-blonde hair back to say something into his ear.

"She's crushing on him," Veronica said.

Lucy squinted at the couple. "She's not even touching him."

Dusty patted Lucy's knee. "That means she likes him."

Lucy was glad when the microphone squealed. She didn't want to have that conversation.

"Welcome to LCSC!" a male voice boomed over the speakers. "Are ya happy?"

While everyone yelled that, yes, they were happy, Carla Rosa reached across Veronica and tugged at Lucy's shorts. "What does LCSC mean?"

"Las Cruces Soccer Camp!" Lucy shouted above the other voices. Only they had all stopped, which meant Lucy's words echoed across the field and up and down the bleachers like she was screaming through a megaphone.

"That's the kind of spirit I'm talkin' about!" the man with the microphone called out. "Everybody—Las Cruces Soccer Camp!"

The crowd yelled it with him—except for Lucy who put her hands up to her burning face. The way the kids around them were staring at her, she wanted to hold up a sign that said, "Yes, I Have the Biggest Mouth in the Mesilla Valley."

But the attention went back to the man on the stage on the other side of the field, who introduced himself as Hawke Somebody. Everybody cheered when he said his first name, and Lucy figured they'd all been to his camp before. She was definitely feeling like the new kid.

Hawke said welcome to the camp and he was glad they were all there and he liked hanging out with soccer players because they were the coolest people in the world. More cheering. Lucy joined in this time, because he was right about that.

"We do have some rules here," he said.

A couple of people booed.

"And one of them is, no booing."

The crowd laughed.

"I'll tell you the rest in just a bit," Hawke said, "but first I want you to get a taste of what you all came here for—and what's that?"

"Soccer!" the crowd yelled.

"What's that—I didn't quite get it."

"Soccer!"

"One more time, and I think I'll have it."

"SOCCER!"

Lucy grinned as she shouted with them. It was definitely her all-time favorite word.

While everyone was still cheering, two teams ran out onto the field, and Hawke announced that they were the winners of last year's camp play-offs, here to inspire the camp with one quarter of exhibition soccer.

Play-offs. Lucy felt another thrill go up her spine. Mr. Auggy had said that was when the ODP people would be there.

She looked around Dusty at J.J. He was forming his own favorite word with his lips: *Sweet*.

A referee in a real uniform, with black socks and everything, blew a whistle, and the game started. A team of all girls was playing a mixed team, and everybody looked like they must be in middle school. Only not *Lucy's* middle school. These kids took their positions behind the center line on each side without looking at each other to make sure they were in the right place like Carla Rosa always did—in spite of all the hours Lucy had spent working with her in her backyard—or redoing their ponytails like Veronica, or punching each other for no reason like Oscar and Emanuel. From the moment a tall girl with muscles in her calves received the ball from the kicker over the center line, they were so intent on the ball, Lucy could almost hear their brains working.

Work the ball sideways and backward till everybody gets into position.

Kick it out to a wing player.

There's too much defense here—get it back to the midfielder.

The team with the ball—the all-girl team—kept it while the offensive players moved into the attacking half of the field. The midfielder sprinted like a deer toward the goal so the wing would have somebody to pass it to. Lucy was a midfielder. She just didn't always have a wing there, since that was supposed to be Veronica.

The other team wasn't making it easy for the all-girl group. Some of the defense was spread out to the wings, but they didn't leave the middle open. They could get the ball anytime, and Lucy hoped they would, just to make it interesting.

One boy tried, running at the girl with the calves to challenge her just as her foot met the ball for a pass. It went wild and bounced out of bounds, and the official blew his whistle.

"Bummer," Dusty said.

Everyone got into position for a goal kick—all except Calf Girl. She marched up to the referee, her face the color of one of Inez's chili peppers, and from the third row, Lucy heard her scream, "That was a foul! He charged me!"

The ref shook his head and waved her back, but she wasn't going anywhere.

"Not fair!" the girl screamed. "He should get carded for that!"

"She's gonna get carded if she doesn't shut up," someone said behind Lucy.

She wasn't sure what a card was, but it couldn't be good. The ref pulled something yellow out of his pocket. Calf Girl swatted it out of his hand.

The whole crowd groaned, the way people did at the movies when the bad guy made his move. Without even opening his mouth, the official pulled another card out, a red one this time. But before the girl could bat that one away, the microphone squealed and every kid in the stands went stone silent. Lucy held her breath.

Hawke's voice boomed low and scary. "Young lady, leave the field, and don't plan to come back."

"I wouldn't play here again if you paid me!" she shouted back. Most of the rest of what she sputtered out was lost as she marched, stiff-legged, off the field. Lucy figured whatever it was couldn't be good.

Before the crowd could start to mutter, Hawke raised his arm. "Soccer is the beautiful game," he said. "It brings people together, teaches them how to work as a team. We reward that at LCSC. Every week, I'll be giving a VIP award. What does that mean?"

"Very Important Player!" the kids who had been there before all yelled.

"And it won't be going to people who behave like that. Or people who come running to me, tattling about every little thing. Or players who can't think of the team instead of themselves. Am I clear?"

He got a huge "yes."

"Then shall we play soccer?"

He got an even huger "yes."

"All right then!"

The whistle blew, and the game started again. All down the third row, Lucy felt the Los Suenos Dreams stiffen as their eyes bulged and their faces went a shade paler. Even Gabe was cracking his knuckles, and she was sure Oscar was about to swallow his toothpick.

"Hey, Team," Lucy hissed at them.

They all leaned toward her.

"We don't do that stuff, so we don't have to worry, okay?"

"What about everybody else, though?" Dusty said. "These people are vicious."

Lucy shook her head. "As long as we're together, we'll be fine."

They nodded at her, and Lucy nodded back. "What's our team motto?"

"What's a motto?" Carla Rosa said.

"The Dreams Don't Die!" Veronica cried, with a wave of her gangly arms.

Yeah, Lucy thought. *That's what I'm talkin' about.*

5

"So, yeah, everybody grab a ball. All except you, Vanessa."

"It's *Veronica*." She giggled at Seth.

Lucy didn't. Coach Seth hadn't gotten anybody's name right all morning, and it was the second day of camp. Mostly he'd been calling them "guys," and if Carla Rosa said, "Guess what? Some of us are girls," one more time, Lucy might scream, except she was pretty sure that was against camp rules.

"Everybody with a ball start juggling it," Seth said out of the only side of his mouth he used.

Oscar tossed the ball in the air with his hands, and Lucy groaned.

"With your feet, Moron," Gabe said.

The whole team said, "Buzz!"

Seth looked at them over the top of his sunglasses. "What's up with that?"

"Our coach buzzes us if we say something mean to somebody," Lucy told him. She wished Coach Auggy was there buzzing like an entire hive of bees right that minute.

"Did somebody say something mean?" Seth shook his head. "Whatever—so, yeah, juggle it with your feet—everybody except Valerie."

"Guess what?" Carla Rosa said. "Her name's Veronica."

"Yeah, well, right now she's the Hunter. She's gonna move around while you're all juggling, waiting for somebody to drop their ball. When somebody does, she's gonna go after it and try to gain control."

Seth looked at Veronica. "That's with your feet only. Then you get to juggle, and whoever you got the ball from becomes the Hunter."

"I don't get it," Oscar said.

"You'll get the hang of it, and then we'll start having the Hunter stay the Hunter with the new Hunter, and the last one left is the winner."

"Now I really don't get it," Oscar said.

Seth blew his whistle. "Start juggling!"

Lucy stepped on her ball, rolled it back and got her foot under it so she could pop it up.

"Guess what?" Carla Rosa whispered. "I forget what juggling is."

She looked like she was about to cry.

"It's like we did at my house," Lucy said as she juggled. "Just toss the ball up with your hands, and then keep it from touching the ground. Then you can only use your feet or your thighs—"

She bounced the ball just above her knee.

"—or your head."

Lucy headed the ball and let it drop until she caught it with her calf and bounced it up again.

"I can't do that!" Carla Rosa said. Her ball fell to the ground, but Veronica the Hunter was busy waiting for Gabe to dump his—which wasn't going to happen. Gabe, Lucy knew, was as good a juggler as she was. Maybe better.

After about five minutes of half the team dropping their balls and Veronica retrieving none of them and Seth missing it all because he was poking at his cell phone, Lucy juggled her way between Gabe and Veronica and purposely let her ball bounce at Veronica's feet.

"Get it," she said.

Veronica let her mouth hang open, and then she squealed and kicked the ball away and trotted off after it.

"Hey, you got one," Seth said. "Now you juggle and Lisa is the Hunter."

Lucy rolled her eyes all the way up into her brain..

Veronica managed to capture the ball with her foot, only to let it roll right to Lucy who danced around it, whispering, "Try again."

"You can start the juggle with your hands first," Seth said.

"Lucy didn't," Veronica said.

Dusty laughed. "That's because Lucy's amazing."

"Are you Lucy?" said someone with a deep voice.

Lucy startled and let the ball get away from her. Two large hands scooped it up. A pair of bright blue eyes sparked at her from over a hooked nose. That must be why they called him Hawke.

"Are you Lucy?" he said again.

Lucy wished she wasn't. His voice boomed even without the microphone. She nodded.

"Coach, I'm taking Lucy."

"Was Lacy the Hunter?" Seth said to the rest of the team.

"Guess what?" Carla Rosa said.

Lucy didn't have to hear the rest. Besides, her thoughts were pounding so loud in her ears, she wouldn't have anyway. Was she about to get busted after only *one* day? And for what? Maybe it was some rule she didn't even know about yet. Red cards dangled before her eyes.

Hawke strode in long-legged steps to a bench at the side of the field where several teams were doing their drills. Anybody between them and the bench stepped aside like Hawke was a king.

"Sit with me," Hawke said to her.

Heart slamming like a screen door, Lucy dropped obediently onto the bench, He put his foot on it and leaned on his knee.

"So you're the famous Lucy," he said.

"Famous?" Lucy said.. How could she be famous already?

"Your coach from Los Suenos—Coach Auggy—isn't that what you call him?"

"Yes." Lucy almost added, "Your Majesty." He even wore his ball cap like a crown over his silver hair.

"He's says you have talent, so I thought I'd come by and see for myself. Do you know what I found out?"

Lucy swallowed and waited for him to go on, but he was obviously expecting an answer.

"The only reason I dropped my ball was because Veronica was never going to get one if I didn't," she said. "She needs the juggling practice."

Hawke's lips parted in a wide smile. "That's exactly what I saw. You're out of there, Lucy."

Lucy was sure all the color was draining from her face, leaving her exactly sixteen freckles to stand alone.

"I was just trying to help her," she said.

"I know. That's why you're out of *there* and on the Girls Select Team."

She knew she was looking stupid, but she could only blink.

"That's the team I've formed from the best I see here at camp," Hawke said. "There's one for boys too. That one's full, which is unfortunate, because I see some others on the Dreams I'd like to include." He pressed his lips out of their smile. "This space opened up when we had to send that player out of camp yesterday."

"Oh," Lucy said.

"Just 'oh?'" Hawke tilted his head at her. "This is a huge opportunity for you, Lucy. This is the team the Olympic Development Program scout will look at. You know about that, right?"

Lucy bobbed her head. "They train players for the Olympics. Only you have to be invited to even try out." She didn't add that she'd already been asked to try out in Texas—only she didn't live there—even though Aunt Karen tried to use that to get Lucy to move there with her. Even in her thoughts she took a deep breath.

"A scout will be here for the play-offs," Hawke said, "and the Select Team will undoubtedly be in the final games."

That did call for more than "oh," but Lucy didn't know what she was supposed to do. She *wanted* to run straight back to the Dreams and tell J.J.—

She froze. This meant she had to be away from the Dreams, away from her team.

"I like this reaction, actually," Hawke said. "You show a lot of humility—that's a good quality in a player."

He let his foot go to the ground and straightened up. He was taller than any man Lucy could ever remember standing next to, which she did now, knees wobbling.

"I'll introduce you to your new team," he said, "and you'll join them right after lunch."

He nodded for her to walk beside him, and she took two steps for each of his, away from the fumbling Dreams, toward a circle of girls who were currently standing around a blonde coach. She was the one Veronica said was "crushing" on Seth. Right now, she appeared to be chewing out her players.

"You were picked for this team because you're superior athletes," she said in a voice that sounded like she was about to have laryngitis. "I haven't seen that so far—"

"Coach Neely," Hawke said.

A smile sprang to her face before she even looked at him. Lucy was sure she had never seen teeth that white. She guessed you didn't show up before Hawke with anything less than perfection.

"I have your new player." Hawke looked down at Lucy. "She just about completes your team. This is Lucy Rooney."

Somebody laughed, although Lucy had never thought there was anything funny about her name. Theirs, when Coach Neely told them all to introduce themselves, went into a puddle in Lucy's head. Bella—Kayla—Patricia—Sarah—Taylor—Waverly.

She hoped there wasn't going to be a test, especially since they were all alike as far as she could tell. Some were Hispanic like Dusty and Veronica, and one seemed to have Native American blood like Januarie, and a few were even white-skinned bolillos like Carla Rosa and her. But something about their faces ran together before her like melting ice cream. She was glad when Coach Neely said, "Time for lunch, girls. I'll meet you back here at one o'clock."

"I have to go get mine," Lucy said, though no one seemed to pay any attention. She ran for the Dreams as if she were going for a goal. If she didn't get back to people whose names she knew, she might forget her own.

She found the team at the picnic table they'd claimed the day before. Nobody had even opened their brown bags yet.

"Did you get busted?" Gabe said—almost as if he certainly hoped so because that would liven things up.

"Of course she didn't." Dusty grabbed Lucy's arm. "You didn't, did you?"

"Guess what?" Carla Rosa said. "They throw you out if you get in trouble, just like that one girl."

"I'm not in trouble!" Lucy said. "I just got moved to another team."

It was hard to sort out all the words and noises that greeted that announcement.

"No, you did not!"

"How come?"

"I don't get it—"

"Do you have to go?"

"Of course she has to go."

Lucy did know who said that, and she stared at J.J. It was a long sentence from him, and not the one she expected.

Gabe poked him. "How do you know, J-man?"

"Just do."

"No you don't." Gabe shrugged. "Not that we can't play without you, Lucy Goosey—"

"Guess what?" Carla Rosa said. "We can't!"

"Maybe *you* can't—"

Dusty buzzed, and Lucy put her hand up. They all muttered into silence.

"I don't want to go," she said. "I'd rather be with you guys—" She looked at Carla Rosa. "—and girls. Maybe I don't have to—I didn't think of that. I could ask Mr. Auggy—"

She felt a nudge in her rib. J.J. was right next to her, jerking his head away from the table. Lucy put her lunch bag down.

"I'll be right back," she said to the team and then followed J.J. to the edge of the pavilion. Behind her, Gabe made a kissing sound.

"You are sick," she heard Dusty say to him.

"What?" Lucy whispered to J.J. when they got to the place where the cement ended.

He lowered his head and talked toward the toes of his tennis shoes. "Don't ask Mr. Auggy if you can change back. You gotta stay on that team."

"Why? I didn't think you'd want me to."

"I don't."

"Then why—"

"Do what that Hawke guy says."

Lucy saw J.J.'s jaw clench down. He was almost done with this conversation, and she still didn't know what he was talking about.

"It's a special team, right?" he said.

"Yeah—and there's one for boys too, and you would totally be on it, only it's full right now—"

"You gotta do it then. Only—"

"Only what?"

J.J. looked up at the acre of picnic tables full of kids. His eyes seemed to get closer together. "Don't talk about our team to those girls. Don't even wear the T-shirt."

"Why?"

"They'll make fun of you."

"What?"

"Pretend you don't even know us."

"I'm not gonna do that, J.J.!" Lucy said. She could feel the exclamation points lining up.

"You get to play real soccer now," J.J. said.

Lucy's throat grew thick. "Are you mad at me?"

"No."

"Are you sure?"

"Yeah."

"J.J.—"

But J.J. was already walking away. The conversation was over.

6

"I used to hate soccer," Januarie announced in the back seat on the way to soccer camp Wednesday morning.

Dusty brushed her finger across Januarie's nose. "Then how come you whined all the time because we wouldn't let you play?"

Lucy could answer that. Januarie just wanted to do what the big kids did, which would have been fine if she had been any good at it.

Veronica stopped braiding her hair and looked at Januarie. "So why don't you hate it anymore?"

"'Cause the people on *my* team are nice to me. *They* don't tell me I don't know how to play."

Lucy was glad J.J. wasn't in their car. He would have said, "You don't."

"And we play with a littler ball, and it's easier." Januarie folded her chubby arms. "It's just way better."

"I wish *I* could say that." Veronica let her lower lip hang. "I don't think I like soccer anymore."

"Really?" said Carla Rosa's mom from behind the steering wheel.

"It's just not that much fun without you, Lucy," Dusty said. "And our coach is kind of—"

"Guess what?" Carla Rosa piped up from the front seat. "He can't even remember our names."

But at least you're all together, Lucy wanted to say. Her coach knew who everybody on their team was, and they all knew each *other.* But the only words that had been spoken to Lucy the afternoon before were Coach Neely saying, "Be sure to drink a lot of water. And wear sunscreen." The rest of the girls acted like all the friend slots were full.

"We still get to eat lunch with you, Bolillo," Dusty said. "Don't we?"

Lucy could hear J.J.'s voice in her head: *Pretend you don't even know us. They'll make fun of you.*

But that couldn't possibly be true. People had to know you were there to make fun of you.

"Don't we?" Dusty said again.

"Try and stop me," Lucy said. And hoped J.J. wouldn't.

Coach Neely started practice with the shoelace pass.

"It's called that because that's exactly the part of the foot you're going to use to kick the ball," she told the Select Team.

"Well, du-uh," said the girl with the ponytail almost to her waist.

Lucy thought she might be Sarah, but whoever she was, nobody buzzed her. Coach Neely just went on with, "It's also called the instep pass. It looks like this."

She took a hop and swung her kicking leg backward, bending it at the knee. As soon as she planted her other foot about three inches from the ball, she swung her kicking leg forward with a snap of her hip. While Lucy soaked it in, Coach Neely pointed her toe down, whacked the center of the ball with the inside of her foot, and sent it skimming down the field. Lucy could feel the power of it, and she imagined a wide-open teammate near the goal, ready to smack it right past the goalie, in front of an ODP scout—

"Yo, Lucy."

Lucy snapped her head up to see Coach Neely peering at her over her sunglasses.

"Why do we do this kick with our instep instead of our toes?"

"You're asking me?" Lucy said.

A girl with what looked like an extra set of teeth snorted.

"Yuk it up, Taylor," Coach Neely said to her. "If she doesn't get it, I'm asking you."

Lucy saw the glint go out of Taylor's narrow black eyes. Everybody else's eyes were on Lucy, and she could feel her cheeks burning.

Coach Neely folded her arms. "Why do we——"

"Because you have more control over where it goes with your instep," Lucy said. "It's harder to get it exactly where you want it with your toe."

Coach Neely blinked. "You're absolutely right."

"I knew that," Taylor said.

The girl next to her, the one with out-of-control hair straining at a headband, poked her. "No, you did not."

Coach Auggy would have been buzzing his head off, but Coach Neely ignored them. "Next question's for you, Patricia."

But before she could ask it, a golf cart puttered up to the edge of their field. Lucy sucked in air when she saw Hawke's silver hair and felt his eyes boring at them as he unfolded himself from the driver's seat.

"Look sharp, girls," Coach Neely said. She plastered on her Hawke-is-here smile.

Hawke stood up—and up and up—while a twelvish girl sprang out of the other seat. She had blonde-streaked light brown hair and eyes that sizzled blue, so Lucy knew she wasn't Hispanic. But the way-long legs that flowed from her shorts and the arms she swung at her sides were as brown as Veronica's. Coach Neely would be telling her to wear sunscreen if she stuck around long enough.

If she did stay, Lucy was pretty sure it was going to be the girl's own choice. She looked at Hawke like he was her manager instead of King Coach, and she didn't fold her arms or twirl her hair around her finger or any of the other things girls did when they entered a new girl-group. Sarah and Taylor whispered behind Lucy:

"Who is *that?*"

"She must be new."

"She has split ends."

Lucy had no idea what that was, but from the pinch of their voices, she knew it couldn't be good. She wondered with a pang if they'd whispered that *her* ends were split yesterday.

"Coach Neely," Hawke boomed out.

"Yes, sir!"

"Your Select Team is complete." He nodded down at the girl, who was now surveying each of them in turn. Nobody seemed to be able to hold her gaze—there was a lot of looking at toes and studying fingernails and examining hair—except Lucy, who couldn't take her eyes off the newcomer. Maybe it was the way she already seemed to be in charge before she'd even said a word.

"This is Rianna Wallace," Hawke said. "She's—"

"I was on a Select Team in Albuquerque," Rianna said, "but I just moved to Alamogordo." She pulled a ponytail holder out of the pocket of her short-sleeved hoodie and scooped her wavy hair into it as she went on. "They don't have one. They don't have anything."

"This team has everything," Hawke said with a broad smile. "You're going to fit right in."

From the way Rianna planted her hands on her hips, it looked like *they'd* better fit in with *her*. Lucy longed to hear a "Guess what?" from Carla Rosa—or even a "Lucy Goosey" from Gabe.

"Let's put the shoelace pass on hold for now," Coach Neely said as Hawke folded himself back into the golf cart and drove off. "Now that we have everybody, we can start gelling as a team. Circle up—we'll play 'Hot Potato.'"

"That's the one where you keep passing the ball around," Rianna said, "and whoever has it when the whistle blows—"

"Is out." Coach Neely gave her a long look before she picked up the ball. Lucy made a note to self: *Don't show off for the coach.* She might have to make a list in her Book tonight to keep track of the rules nobody said out loud.

"That's not the way we played it in Albuquerque," Rianna said. Everybody gaped at her. "The way we did it was every time you get caught with the ball, you get a letter in the word POTATO. The first one who spells the whole word is out. It lasts longer that way."

She held out her arms and wiggled her fingers at Coach Neely. "I'll start."

Taylor gave a nervous-sounding snort. "So which way are we playing it?"

"My way," Coach Neely said, and passed the ball to a tiny girl with a boy-short haircut. "You start, Kayla. Girls, spread out your circle and use as many different passes as you can. The point is to learn to vary your passes. And don't forget to talk to each other."

"What's your name?" Rianna said, blue eyes drilling into Kayla.

"Kay—"

"To me, Kay."

To Lucy's surprise, little Kayla's pass was crisp and sure, though she made it right to Rianna as instructed. Rianna made a push pass so hard at Sarah that she practically fell backward trapping it. Before she could even plant her foot, Rianna was saying, "Back to me!"

Sarah-of-the-Long-Ponytail looked at Coach Neely, but she was taking a swig out of her water bottle.

"To *me!*" Rianna yelled.

Sarah gave the ball a shove, but her foot hit it on the bottom instead of in the center, and the ball popped up and landed several feet short of Rianna. She made a hissing sound as she ran up on it, already looking around. Her eyes stopped on Lucy.

"To you!" she said, and lofted a pass Lucy had to trap with her chest. She heard Rianna shout, "Now back to me!" But the hair on the back of Lucy's neck was standing up. Who resigned and made her coach? Lucy let the ball drop and glanced at the girl next to her—the one with the wild hair—was her name Patricia?

"To you," Lucy said, and used the outside of her foot to give the ball a nice nudge.

"What was that?" Rianna said.

"That was a good move!" Coach Neely said. "Pass it, Patricia!"

Patricia took her time—which got the veins in Rianna's forehead bulging—and made a controlled pass across the circle to a girl Lucy hadn't seen smile yet.

"To you, Waverly," Patricia said, *after* she kicked the ball.

"Aw, man!" Rianna said.

Waverly missed the pass, but she managed to retrieve the ball, and Lucy was impressed that she didn't take the time to turn around but made a heel pass instead.

"Nice!" Coach Neely said.

The ball came straight to Lucy, and she scanned the circle to see who hadn't had a chance yet. A Hispanic girl with two braids looked back at her hopefully.

"To you-with-the-braids," Lucy said, and lobbed the ball her way. Coach Neely did say to use different kinds of passes.

"Hold your foot up, Bella!" Coach Neely called to her.

Bella appeared to be ready — until another figure was suddenly there between her and the ball. Rianna headed it, bounced it off of her thigh, and planted it on the ground. Coach Neely blew the whistle.

"You're out, Rianna," she said.

"Why?"

"Because I just blew the whistle and you have the ball."

Across the circle, Lucy saw Sarah put her hand over her mouth. Next to her, she heard Patricia mutter, "Serves you right."

Lucy waited for Rianna to pitch a fit. As visions of the girl who got thrown out of camp went through her mind, she almost wished she would.

But Rianna shrugged and backed out of the circle. The second Coach Neely gave the ball to Bella, Rianna bent forward, hands on her knees, ponytail dangling over her shoulder, mouth going.

She pointed at Waverly. "Pass it to her!"

Bella obeyed, but this time, Waverly was ready and passed it on first touch. These girls were good.

But obviously not good enough for Rianna, who paced around the circle like somebody's embarrassing father, yelling—

"That was a lazy pass!"

"Who were you passing to? You were way off!"

"Hit it in the middle, not the top!"

When Coach Neely finally blew the whistle, Kayla looked grateful that she had the ball and squinted her already tiny eyes at Rianna as she left the circle. Sarah shot up her hand.

"Question?" Coach Neely said.

"Yeah." Sarah stuck her gaze on Rianna. "Who's the coach?"

"I am," Coach Neely said. "So why don't you let me deal with it?"

"Then, like, do it," Patricia muttered.

Lucy nodded at her. One more thing to add to that Unspoken Rules List: *Let the coach handle everything. Including girls that think they run the whole world.*

At lunchtime, Lucy snatched up her backpack and walked, stiff-legged-fast, toward the Dreams' table. She couldn't get away from Rianna's voice fast enough. She was sure it was taking over her brain, so when she heard it behind her calling, "Hey—Freckle Girl," she looked over her shoulder to assure herself Rianna wasn't really there. Big mistake.

"Yeah—you," Rianna said.

She reached Lucy in two more long-legged leaps and grabbed onto Lucy's backpack like she knew she wanted to take the nearest escape route. She was smart, this girl.

"Eat lunch with me," Rianna said close to Lucy's ear.

"I usually eat with—"

"Forget them."

Rianna jerked her head toward the rest of the Select Team who were already gathered at a table, heads almost touching as they chattered. Lucy could guess the topic.

"I just want to talk to *you*," Rianna said.

"I promised my—"

"No, seriously." Rianna got her face so close, Lucy could feel her hot breath. "We have to talk about this team. Over there." She pointed to one of the cottonwood trees that bordered the soccer park and strode off toward it.

Lucy didn't follow her. Rianna might think she was the boss of the team, but she wasn't the boss of Lucy. She whipped around to head for her friends and almost plowed into J.J.

"Man, am I glad to see you," she said. "You would not believe what's going on. Come on—we'll talk at the table."

"I already told 'em you weren't comin'."

Lucy stopped, jaw unhinging. "Why?"

"What I told you."

"I don't care if the team makes fun of me," Lucy said. She lowered her voice to a hiss and nodded toward the tree, where Rianna was running off two seven-year-olds. "Especially her."

"Eat with your team," J.J. said.

"I don't want to. I want to be with you guys." Her words grew thick. "My team doesn't even know I'm not there."

"So tell 'em."

"I don't get this." Lucy stared hard at J.J. "You never care about people teasing you."

"I care about 'em teasin' *you.*"

His voice shot high on the "you," and his face went the color of a tomato, and his Adam's apple bobbed three times. He backed away, shaking his head, though Lucy knew better than to say anything else anyway.

"Don't come," he said, and slipped away through a clump of boys.

"Hey!" said that voice Lucy was sure she'd be hearing in her sleep.

"I gotta go!" Lucy called to her.

Then she ran to the restroom and slipped past two girls redoing their French braids in the mirrors and hid in a stall, staying there long after they finished whispering about how weird she was acting and left. *She* was the one who was weird? What about Rianna, who was behaving like she was the boss of her when Lucy couldn't even remember her last name? What about J.J., who must have just had a personality transplant or something? How was she *supposed* to act when everybody else was going crazy?

She didn't know, so she stayed in the stall until lunch time was over.

Coach Neely divided them into two teams that afternoon and had them play a practice game. Lucy said a major prayer of thanks that Rianna was her team's goalie so she didn't have to deal with her too much. At least when she was playing soccer, Rianna didn't talk about anything else. The rest of the team, on the other hand...

Maybe it was the heat that made everybody cranky, but Lucy heard everything from Sarah telling Waverly she wanted to stuff the ball up Rianna's nose, to Patricia muttering that flushing her down the toilet would be better. Coach Neely didn't say anything, at least not about Rianna. She had plenty to say about how they were all talented individual athletes, but they needed to learn to play as a team.

Lucy *knew* how to play as a team. But maybe this wasn't the team she was supposed to be on.

7

As soon as camp was over for the day, Lucy bolted for the car, only to slow down as she got closer and saw Dusty and the other girls piling in. They probably weren't going to talk to her after she had ditched them at lunch. And what was *she* supposed to say to *them?*

J.J. hadn't told her what to do about that.

With a sigh that came all the way from her shoelaces, Lucy made her way to Carla Rosa's SUV. Dusty was the only one who hadn't gotten in, and she wrapped her arms around Lucy's neck.

"I'm so sorry," she said.

"About what?" Lucy said.

"You know—that your coach is making you eat with your team."

As much as she hated long hugs, Lucy was glad Dusty was still holding onto her so she couldn't see her eyes bugging out.

"We understand," Dusty said.

Veronica poked her head out the window. "We know we're your *real* friends."

Carla Rosa joined her, cheeks nearly purple from the heat. "Guess what, though? You didn't eat with them either. How come you didn't eat?"

"Get in, girls," Carla's mom said from the driver's seat. "Lucy, you didn't have lunch today?"

"I wasn't hungry," Lucy said. And that was the truth. This whole thing was taking away her appetite.

It came back, though, after a ride back to Los Suenos with friend-voices, voices that weren't Rianna's. The cheesy aroma of Inez's chili *rellenos* when she walked in the back door helped too. And knowing she was going to eat with Dad sealed it: she was starving for food and for the chance to tell him everything that was happening so he could help her sort it out. He was very cool that way, even if he'd never kicked a soccer ball in his life.

But when she rode the yellow Navajo rug to the kitchen after her shower, Mr. Auggy was at the table, eyeing the bubbling *rellenos*. Normally that would have made the evening perfect, but he had a book on the table next to him that said something on the cover about improving reading skills.

"Now there's a look I haven't seen in a while," Coach Auggy said, smiling his small smile at her.

Dad pointed his face toward Lucy. "What look is that?"

"It's the 'I hate schoolwork in the summer' look." Lucy dropped into her chair. "No offense, Mr. Auggy."

"None taken. But who said it had to be *work*? Or *school*, for that matter?"

"We're going to 'improve my reading skills.'" Lucy made quotation marks with her fingers the way Mora always did. "That sounds like schoolwork to me."

"Let's watch our tone, Luce," Dad said.

"Sorry," Lucy said. She didn't add that after the day she'd had, she was doing well not to throw tortillas.

"Apology accepted." Mr. Auggy took a bite of *rellenos* and closed his eyes. Inez's cooking did require stopping and savoring, no matter what else was going on. "I know they serve this in heaven," he said. "Okay, so, captain, which one of your cats is the most intellectual?"

"The most what?"

"If they were human kids, which one would do the best in school?"

Lucy picked a chili out with her fork. It was always best to test one before you took a whole mouthful. Inez sometimes forgot the

Rooneys didn't have hot-ready taste buds like the Herreras. Besides, that question required some thought.

"Definitely not Mudge," she said finally. "He'd be more like the playground bully."

Dad gave his sandpaper chuckle. "I'd have to agree with that."

"And not Lolli. She'd be all girly and worried about her clothes and stuff." She took a bite and chewed thoughtfully. "Probably not Artemis Hamm either. I bet she'd play soccer like me."

"So that leaves what's-his-nose." Mr. Auggy nodded at Marmalade who was curled up in the chair next to Dad. "You think he'd be a good student?"

"Marmalade?" Dad laughed. "I think he'd sleep through all of his classes."

But Lucy shook her head. "He hangs out with you all the time, Dad. That means he's gotta be smart."

Something soft passed over Dad's face, like she'd just given him a homemade Father's Day present he was going to keep forever.

"How come you want to know that anyway?" Lucy said to Mr. Auggy.

His small smile got bigger. "I thought you'd never ask. I found out about this program where they train dogs to go into schools and sit with kids while they read out loud to them."

"O-kay," Lucy said.

"Think about it. If you read to Marshmallow over there—"

"Marmalade!"

"Is he going to say things like, 'Dude, where did you learn to read?' or 'Uh, that's *these*, not *those*'?"

Lucy shook her head.

"So if you're reading him a story, about catnip or mice or whatever, and he just purrs in your lap, you're going to feel pretty good about your audience, right?"

It would definitely be better than having Carla Rosa saying "Guess what? That was wrong" or Oscar pretending to snore. And who knew what the kids in middle school were going to say when she got all nervous and stumbled over words like rocks in the dark? Not a pretty thought.

"I figure a cat can be as good as a dog—" Mr. Auggy said.

"Well, of *course!*"

"So I thought we'd try it. What would you like to start off with?"

Lucy blinked. "Are you serious? I get to pick what I want to read?"

"Sure. Right now it doesn't matter so much *what* you read as *that* you read. A half hour a day." Mr. Auggy nodded at Marmalade again. "You think you can get old Jelly Belly to sit still that long?"

"I definitely think he's your man," Dad said.

"I don't know what to read, though," Lucy said. "I've never exactly read for fun."

"I thought as much." Mr. Auggy reached under the boring looking book at his elbow and pulled out one with kids—hello!—playing soccer on the front. *The Everything Kids' Soccer Book.* "You think Marmaduke would be interested in this?"

Lucy didn't even correct him this time. She just took the book and held it reverently.

"What's our topic?" Dad said.

"Soccer," Lucy whispered.

"Why did I even have to ask?"

Dad was smiling, but his grin faded as he took a few bites from his plate. Lucy looked at Mr. Auggy. He was looking suddenly serious about his supper too.

"Okay," Lucy said. "What's the catch?"

"What makes you think there's a catch?" Coach Auggy said.

"My champ is perceptive," Dad said.

Lucy didn't know what that was, but her stomach did a nervous flutter thing. She should have known it was too good to be true.

"There's something else we want to talk to you about, Luce," Dad said. "You know I went to the Town Council meeting last night—and we discussed the soccer field."

Lucy put the book down and got up on one knee. "They're going to fix it, aren't they?"

"That's one idea."

"That's the only idea!"

Dad looked as though the chili *rellenos* had gone sour.

"Some of the business owners in town have been approached again by the big corporation that wants to buy the field." Mr. Auggy's said. His small smile was now far away.

"The people that want to put a stupid mini-mart there?" Lucy said.

"They've talked to Felix Pasco and Mr. Benitez and Claudia and Gloria, saying they—the corporation—will put money into the the café and the grocery store and the flower shop and the beauty salon in exchange for their votes on the council to sell the field."

Lucy got on *both* knees. "But they can't do that, can they?"

Both Dad and Mr. Auggy nodded sadly.

"We just want you to know that some of them are considering changing their votes," Dad said.

"What?" Lucy cried. "I thought they were proud of the team!"

"It isn't that they're not, but times are hard, Luce. People have to keep their businesses going or they can't pay their bills."

It looked to Lucy as if her Dad had a sudden pain. Mr. Auggy was trying to smile, but Lucy didn't believe it was for real.

"Nothing has been decided yet," Mr. Auggy said. "But we thought you should know what's going on."

"It's something we have to pray about," Dad said. "Things are changing, and we need to be ready."

Nobody said anything for a minute, although Lucy's silence was louder than anyone's. She didn't want 'change', and she had no intention of getting ready for it.

Mr. Auggy finally cleared his throat. "Meanwhile, you and Marmalade—did I get it right that time?" He managed to get a grin going. "You two can dive into that soccer book. For the time being, you do have a field to play on at camp. How's that going for you?"

"Fine," Lucy lied. She stood up and scooped Marmalade and the soccer book into her arms. "Could I be excused, Dad?"

"You okay, champ?" he said.

"Yes," she said.

As she escaped to her room, she thought that she was sure doing a lot of lying right now.

Once she was there, she didn't feel much like reading to Marmalade, but she did hold him on her lap as she slipped the Book of Lists out from under her pillow and wrote.

Dear God:

What Am I Supposed To Do About All This Stuff?

1. How am I supposed to keep Felix and Mr. Benitez and all those people from selling our soccer field?
2. How am I gonna stand being on the Select Team with Rianna in my face all the time? And Coach Neely not doing anything about it? And nobody else on the team even talking to me?
3. How can I convince J.J. that it doesn't matter if they make fun of me? I want to be with MY team!!!!!!!!

Marmalade didn't even seem to notice the exclamation points. Not like Lollipop who was flicking a jealous tail up on the windowsill.

4. What if Marmalade doesn't help me learn to read better? What if I don't do it right?
5. How do I get that sad look off of Dad's face? Because it's way too worried for just me "improving my reading skills" or even us losing our field.

Lucy rubbed at her nervous stomach with her pen. She knew her dad. He always said God could help them through anything. He didn't get that maybe-even-God-can't-this-time worry in his eyes unless something was way wrong.

Things are changing, and we need to be ready, he'd told her.

What else could possibly change? What exactly was he getting ready for?

Lucy hugged the Book and checked out the window for a possible J.J. signal and made exclamation points in Marmalade's fur with her finger. But nothing took away the dread that clung to her like a cobweb. The one thing that always helped was soccer. And now, she wasn't even looking forward to that.

But things started off better the next day at camp. Coach Neely divided the team in half, and Lucy nearly cheered when Rianna ended up on the other side. She was looking pretty grumpy and didn't have much to say to anybody, but Lucy had a feeling that was going to change, and she didn't want to be on the other end of it.

Lucy stood in a line with Bella-with-the-braids, Sarah-of-the-long-ponytail, and tiny Kayla and tried to concentrate on what Coach Neely was saying. It was a little hard with Patricia-with-the-out-of-control-hair muttering under her breath like she never stopped doing and toothy Taylor and Waverly-no-smile glaring at Rianna and Rianna glaring back. Lucy decided she had the better team. At least they didn't look like they wanted to eat each other.

"Lucy's side is going to have four balls," Coach Neely said. "Rianna's side will have none."

"How come?" Rianna said.

"Why are we called 'Rianna's side'?" Taylor said.

Coach Neely parked her ball on one hip. "This is the reason we're doing this exercise," she said. "You girls have to start talking *to* each other instead of *about* each other. When you're out on the field in a game, you can't depend on me to tell you what to do. You have to rely on one another, which is why I didn't stop Rianna from 'coaching' you yesterday." She didn't appear to see Rianna looking like she'd just scored a goal—or hear Patricia muttering or Taylor snorting. "At least somebody was talking. Now, here's the way this game works—"

Within a few minutes, Lucy's side was dribbling around the area Coach Neely marked off. Whenever they heard someone on Rianna's side call their name, they had to pass their ball to that player and run off and find someone with a ball who they could call to.

Lucy's name was called a lot. When she had to call, it was hard not to say, "Long Ponytail!" or "Toothy!" She was amazed that by the time Coach Neely blew her whistle, she finally knew everybody's name. She just wished Rianna didn't know hers.

When Coach Neely had them sit down and drink water while she explained the next thing, Rianna maneuvered herself to sit right next to Lucy. Lucy was afraid she was going to start in about lunch yesterday, but Rianna smiled—a sort of curled-lip smile—and scooted in close.

"What I just saw on the field," Coach Neely said, "that's what I'm talkin' about." She flashed her very white teeth in a rare smile. "I think you're getting the idea. Now, let's work on strategy. We'll start with when you should dribble instead of passing or shooting—"

"I already know that," Rianna whispered to Lucy. "I bet you do too."

Lucy nodded and kept her eyes frozen to Coach Neely.

"If you're all by yourself and no one is challenging you, by all means dribble."

"Like a mad dog," Mr. Auggy would have said. Lucy felt a pang of homesickness.

"Take as much of the field as the defenders will give you."

Rianna poked Lucy. "Which isn't going to be much if we're the defenders, right?"

"If the defenders do approach you, what are your options?"

The girls called out things like, "Send the ball to an open player," and "Do a wall pass." Rianna put her lips close to Lucy's ear and said, "Fall down."

Lucy pulled her gaze from Coach Neely and stared at her.

"Later," Rianna whispered.

It was hard to soak in the rest of what Coach Neely said, with *fall down* racing through her brain. Did Rianna mean on purpose? Why would she want to do that? Nah, there was no way that's what she meant.

"We'll work on this stuff in our practice game this afternoon," Coach Neely said. "Have a good lunch."

Lucy hurried to join the Select Team at the table this time, before

Rianna could try to drag her off alone. She was just settling in between Kayla and Bella, since they seemed like the least likely to torture her with their eyes, when Patricia leaned across the table and muttered something.

"Don't you even know how to talk out loud like a normal person?" Rianna said.

Patricia just muttered again. It sounded like *Lucysomeguywantsto-talktoyou*. Lucy looked back over her shoulder and saw J.J. jerking his head at her.

"Is that your boyfriend?" Sarah said.

Taylor gave her signature snort. "He's cute."

"Tell him to come over here," Rianna said.

Lucy scrambled out of her seat before Rianna could beat her to it. She really didn't want to see what would happen if Rianna did her pushy thing with J.J.

Her thoughts tumbled over each other in a confused mess as she hurried to him. First he tells her not to even talk about him and the rest of the Dreams to her new team. Now he calls her out when she's right in the middle of them. What was up with that?

The moment Lucy got close to him, she knew why. His skin pinched around his eyes, and his jaw clenched like he'd just tightened it with a screwdriver.

"Did somebody get hurt?" she said when she got to him. "Is it Januarie? Did she get in trouble?"

J.J. didn't even bother to shake his head as he led her behind the restroom building, out of sight of her team. Lucy's stomach tied itself into a knot. Was she going to have to add something else to the list she'd made last night?

"What is going *on*, J.J.?" she said. "You're scaring me."

"I heard something," he said. "Something bad. And I think you're the only one who can fix it."

8

I can't! Lucy wanted to scream at J.J. *I can't even fix the stuff I already have on my list!!!!*

She was still adding exclamation points as J.J. looked over both shoulders, his Adam's apple bobbing.

"What did you hear, J.J.?" she said.

"I left my backpack in the parking lot this morning—"

"Why?"

"By mistake."

"Oh."

"These two girls were talking by a car. They didn't see me."

"What were they talking about?"

"Cheating."

"In soccer?"

"The one girl told the other one she knew ways to do it."

"That's ridiculous, J.J. How are you gonna cheat in soccer?" Even as Lucy said the words, she heard Rianna's in her ear: *Fall down.*

"I don't know," J.J. said. The *know* shot up into another octave. "But the other one said she'd do it to show him."

"Show who what?"

"She didn't say *what.* She just said *who.*" J.J. shifted his eyes around again before he said, "Hawke."

"Somebody wants to show *Hawke* something?"

"Yeah. She sounded like the girl that got kicked out."

"Who was the other one?"

"I didn't see her."

Lucy shook her head. "So, how do you think *I'm* gonna fix this, J.J.?"

"You have to tell Hawke."

"Me!"

"He knows you."

"But I'm not the one who heard this whole thing."

J.J.'s eyes narrowed. "You don't believe me?"

"Of course I believe you, but Hawke said he didn't want people tattling, remember?"

A whistle blew, and J.J. backed away. "Seth gets mad if we're late. We gotta think of something."

You mean I have to think of something, Lucy wanted to say. She turned to go.

"This is why," J.J. said.

"This is why what?"

"These kids are mean. Meaner than in Los Suenos. This is why you gotta protect yourself. "

Then he was gone. Lucy swallowed hard and went back to some of those mean kids. She would have been happier going to take an English test—and that was the last thing she ever wanted to do.

"Same teams as yesterday," Coach Neely said when they were all there. "But let's switch goalies. Waverly, you take Rianna's place. Taylor, you're in for Patricia."

Lucy groaned inside. That meant she would have to play with Rianna. She would rather be the ball and get kicked around.

The good thing was that people remembered to talk to each other, and Two-Braid Bella, who never talked much otherwise, turned out to be very good at it. By calling the right passes, she got Rianna into the penalty box with a great chance to score. But Patricia and Kayla were "smokin' defenders," as Coach Neely called them, and Rianna found herself with no place to go.

"To me!" Lucy shouted.

Instead, Rianna was suddenly on the ground, holding her ankle and scrunching up her face. The ball bounced away, and Patricia and

Kayla looked at each other like Rianna was speaking Swahili. Coach Neely blew her whistle and called a foul.

Lucy saw Patricia's lips move, but of course she couldn't hear what she was saying. Kayla looked tinier than ever and merely blinked at Coach Neely.

"You okay?" Coach called to Rianna.

"I think so." Rianna motioned to Lucy. "Help me up."

"What happens when a foul occurs in the penalty box, ladies?" Coach Neely asked as Lucy dragged herself over.

"Penalty kick," Bella said.

"Then let's get set up."

Lucy squatted beside Rianna. Before she could ask if she was all right—only because it was the polite thing to do—Rianna whispered, "See how that works?"

"How what works?" Lucy whispered back.

"Flopping. We get a free kick out of it."

Lucy felt herself go cold inside. She stood up without giving Rianna her hand.

Rianna struggled to her feet, wincing like a TV actor. "It's easy when there's only one official," she said near Lucy's ear. "Don't try it in this game since I already did—"

"Rianna—are you going to take the kick or not?"

"Can Lucy do it for me? My ankle really hurts."

As if to prove it, Rianna limped over to the touchline and sank back to the ground. "I'll be okay if I just sit here for a minute," she said.

Coach Neely rubbed her own forehead. "All right—Lucy, take the kick."

But it wasn't fair. Rianna should be the one getting a penalty. Lucy marched toward Coach Neely, but something caught her waistband. She looked down to see Kayla tugging at her.

"Just take the kick," she said in a voice as tiny as she was.

"But she—"

"Don't mess with her. She won't get away with it in a real game anyway."

Coach Neely straightened from inspecting Rianna's ankle and tossed the ball to Lucy, who felt like she'd just shoplifted from Mr. Benitez's store. If she scored for her team this way, it was as bad as if she was the one who'd faked being fouled. And there was a good chance she would score. A penalty kick was a free kick 12 yards from the goal line, with no defenders inside the penalty box. Only Taylor the goalie stood in her way, and Lucy knew she could fake her out.

But when Coach Neely blew the whistle, Lucy kicked the ball right to her. Taylor looked so surprised she almost missed it before she scooped the ball easily into her hands and put it back into play.

Lucy didn't look at Rianna. She didn't have to. She could feel her eyes drilling holes through her.

As soon as camp was over that day, Lucy raced to find Mr. Auggy. J.J. was wrong. She couldn't fix this, but their coach could.

She located him on the junior boys' field where a pack of seven-and eight-year-olds were still smacking the ball around and calling for "Coach A" to "Watch this!" while he called back that it "really is time to leave, guys." When he spotted Lucy, he made them all get their stuff and scoot.

"What's up, captain?" he said. "You okay?"

Lucy wiped the sweat from her upper lip and shook her head.

"You're not having fun on the Select Team?"

"No."

To Lucy's dismay, she felt tears threatening at the back of her throat. If she cried, it would just look like she was being a whiner. He had enough of that with Januarie.

She swallowed hard. "There's this one girl," she said. "I think she's trying to get me to gang up with her against the rest of the team—and I'm not sure, but I think she—well, she fell down today, and I don't think it was—"

She stopped, becauseMr. Auggy was shaking his head at her. Mr. Auggy, who always listened.

"Sorry, captain," he said. "But this sounds like girl drama. I know the girls on our team are done with that, but this is a new group—"

"It isn't just that!"

78

He smiled his small smile and motioned for her to walk with him. "I think you ought to talk to Coach Neely about this."

"Coach Neely likes this girl! She doesn't say anything to her when she's bossy, and she's all concerned about her ankle—"

"Coach Neely's good. She's more hands-off than what you're used to with me, but she'll listen."

Which was more than he was doing right now. Lucy's eyes stung with disappointment.

"Speaking of coaches, I have a meeting," he said. "But you talk to her tomorrow, okay?"

And say what? Lucy thought as she dragged herself toward the waiting car. If she told Coach Neely she thought Rianna was trying to cheat, would she even believe her? Rianna could say the same thing about *her*—and Coach at least paid attention to Rianna, especially now that she was all worried about her injury.

No, J.J. was wrong. She wasn't the person to try to fix this.

Besides, the next day, Friday, Rianna didn't show up for camp.

"Did Rianna drop out?" Sarah asked Coach Neely. Lucy heard the hope in her voice.

"I told her she had to have a doctor's note before she could come back," Coach said. "Camp rule for liability reasons. She's probably having her ankle checked out."

"I hope that appointment takes all day," Patricia muttered.

Lucy smothered a smile.

"Don't let Coach Neely hear you say that," Sarah whispered as they gathered to pull soccer balls out of the bag.

"Why?" Waverly said.

Taylor snorted. "Because Rianna's her pet."

"I hate it when coaches have pets," little Kayla said. "Ours does in Cloudcroft."

"Yeah, well, this one thinks she, like, has a pedigree or something." Sarah flipped her long ponytail. "I wish somebody would put her on leash."

Lucy felt a little better. At least she had one thing in common with her team. Too bad it had to be we-all-despise-Rianna.

The "pet" appeared at the lunch break, without a leash, waving her doctor's note and hopping up and down on her foot to show that she'd been miraculously cured. Lucy made her usual beeline, but Rianna got in front of her before she could even pick up her backpack.

"You messed up that free kick on purpose yesterday," she said, instead of "hi."

Lucy blinked at her and said, "Huh?" Rianna wasn't the only one who could act.

Rianna pulled her off the field by her sleeve, smiling as if she were about to share some girl secret with her. Coach Neely grinned at them before she turned to flash her very white smile at Seth.

"You know what I'm talking about," Rianna said when the two coaches were gone. "Look, they call us the Select Team, but let's face it, me and you are the only ones that really deserve that name."

"Everybody's good," Lucy said. She tried to pull away, but Rianna held on tighter to her shirt.

"They're good, but they're not great. You know we're the team the ODP is gonna look at, don't you?"

They weren't going to look at cheaters.

Lucy wanted to say that. She even opened her mouth to let the words out. But Rianna squeezed harder and caught some of Lucy's skin in her fingers.

"You don't know how they play in the big cities," she said through her teeth. "It's dirty out there. I'm just telling you this because I like you: you can't be a goody-goody rule-follower or they'll run right over you. I've had girls trip me and pinch me and grab my clothes, and they get away with it. You have to learn to fight back."

She finally let go of Lucy's arm, but Lucy didn't move. If she answered, that would mean this was real—and she so didn't want it to be.

"I can either be your best friend or your worst enemy," Rianna said. "And you don't want me for your enemy."

That was the first thing she said that Lucy thought was absolutely true. She waited until she could breathe again before she followed Rianna to the lunch table.

They didn't play a practice game that afternoon because it was blistering hot. Lucy was grateful for that. But she still felt prickly all over when she got home, the same way she did when she was sitting in the dentist's waiting room.

Inez greeted her with Lucy's favorite warm *sopapillas* and honey and her Bible.

"I'm so bored, even Bible study sounds good," Mora said. "Go figure."

Inez folded her hands on her open Bible. "Today there is *buenos noticias* for Senorita Esther."

"That means 'good news,'" Mora said.

Lucy didn't have the energy to be annoyed. Mora looked disappointed.

"Senor King, he loves Senorita Esther from the moment he lays his eyes on her."

Mora slapped the table. "I knew it."

"She will be the queen."

Good for her. Lucy wished somebody would make her queen. The first thing she'd do would be to banish Senorita Rianna from the kingdom. Then buy the Los Suenos soccer field. Then put all her friends on the Select Team with her. Then she'd wipe out cheating—

"What is *wrong* with you?"

Lucy looked up at Mora, who was staring at Lucy's hands, with good reason. Lucy had ripped her sopapilla into tiny pieces on her plate.

Inez was watching her too, but she just said, "We go on," and ran her finger down the page. "Queen Esther, she still misses her *amigas*, and still she cannot say she is the Jew."

"Yeah, but she's got the Hot Hottie from Hottsville," Mora said. "What more does she want?"

"Senor Cousin Mordecai, he visits her every day," Inez continued.

"This brings Senorita Esther the comfort. And he tells her the important things to do."

Mora grunted. "What does she need him for? She's the queen."

Inez put up a finger. "The queen cannot know everything. Senor Mordecai, he tells her two evil guards, they will kill the Senor King."

Lucy got up on one knee. "How does he know?"

"He hears their plan."

"Why didn't he tell the king himself? I would." Mora wiggled her eyebrows. "Then maybe he'd notice me and—"

"He didn't think the king would believe him, right?" This was all sounding so familiar, it was giving Lucy goose bumps.

"This is right," Inez said. "So Senora Queen Esther, she goes to the king, and she tells him—and she says to him that Senor Mordecai was the one give her this information. Senor King is most grateful."

"I bet he was." Mora sighed with drama. "I bet he bought her, like, a bunch of jewelry—a Lexus—oh, wait, they didn't have cars—"

Lucy slumped back in her chair. This was definitely like her situation with J.J. and the whole cheating thing. But she wasn't a queen, and King Hawke wasn't likely to be "most grateful" unless she had proof.

Inez had by now closed her Bible and was busy at the sink with Lucy and Dad's dinner. Mora opened her cell phone and poked at the keys with her thumbs the way she was always doing. Lucy watched, uninterested, until something occurred to her.

"Does that have a camera?" Lucy said.

Mora gave her a blank look. "Of course it does."

"Can you take, like, movies with it? Like even when people don't know it?"

"Oh, yeah, see—" Mora stopped and lifted an eyebrow at Lucy. "Why?"

Lucy glanced at Inez's back and then at Mora. When she nodded toward the back door, Mora's eyes took on a gleam.

"We're going outside, Abuela," Mora said, way too casually, and herded Lucy out onto the steps.

"Okay, I know you're planning something, Lucy," she said before the door was even closed. "It's all over your face. And by the way, don't start trying to make it as a sneak. You'll never pull it off."

Lucy opened her mouth, but the words stayed crowded in her throat. Was she actually about to get Mora to help her with some scheme when Mora's little plans always ended up making everything worse that they were to start with? Lucy shoved the whole idea back down where it came from and shrugged. "I'm being stupid. Forget it."

"Oh, no you don't." Mora folded her arms and wiggled her head. "You have no idea how boring it is around here — except when I'm at dance class — with everybody off at soccer camp. Abuela lets me watch way more TV than usual, but even I can only take so much *Days of Our Lives*, if you know what I mean."

Lucy didn't.

Mora leaned forward, cell phone in hand. "Let me help you with this plan of yours — please — before I go nuts."

"I don't have a plan," Lucy said.

"I could help you think of one." Mora slanted her eyes. "I can be very crafty."

"I know," Lucy said, rolling hers. "But things are 'crafty' enough already."

"All right," Mora said. "But if I die of boredom, it's going to be your fault."

Great. That was one more thing to add to the list of stuff she was supposed to do something about.

Maybe, just maybe, she would rather be bored.

9

"How's Marmalade doing with his reading?" Dad asked Lucy Sunday afternoon as she was headed out the back door to practice her dribbling. Dad had gotten her a new ball after the storm—with Mr. Auggy's help—and she wanted to try it out.

She leaned on the screen and tucked it under her arm. "He's not doing that well."

"I'm surprised. I thought he'd be a prime candidate for sitting on your lap."

"Um, I haven't exactly been making that much of a lap for him to sit in."

Dad's eyebrows went up. "And that would be because . . . ?"

Because every time she sat down to read, all she could think about was all the stuff on her list that she couldn't do anything about. When she read the list to Marmalade, Lucy got dentist's-office prickly and ended up pacing around the room, or sending signals to J.J.

"I have a lot on my mind," she said to Dad.

He took a sip from his lemonade and made a sour face, although Lucy knew Inez put plenty of sugar in her recipe.

"Funny how getting lost in a book can take a person's mind off of problems," he said. "I miss that."

Lucy wanted to swallow her soccer ball. She usually tried pretty hard not to make Dad sad about his blindness, but sometimes she plowed right in and did it anyway. Standing up straighter, she made her voice go cheerful. "You know what?" she said. "Maybe I'll go in and try it."

"That's my champ," Dad said.

It wasn't going to work, she was sure of that as she picked up a sleepy Marmalade and skimmed to her room on the yellow rug. But if it didn't, she wasn't going to get to play soccer anyway.

She plopped the kitty on her bed and flopped down beside him.

"That's called *flopping*," Rianna had said to her. Lucy grunted. It was one thing to do it on your mattress and another to use it to cheat in soccer.

Lucy sat up. Could there possibly be something about cheating in that book Mr. Auggy gave her? Where did she put it anyway?

She flipped her head upside-down to peer under the bed and found Lolli curled up on it. She yowled indignantly as Lucy pried the thing out.

"You can come up and be read to, too," Lucy told her.

Another protest. It was obviously too much, having to share the bedroom with Marmalade.

Lucy sat cross-legged against her pillows and didn't have to do much coaxing to get Marmalade to join her. Finding anything to do with cheating in the book was a lot harder. There was nothing in the table of contents, and a flip-through didn't pop out anything. She was about to give up when she caught the words FOUL PLAY in bold letters with a frowny face next to them.

"This could be it, Marmie," she said.

She was rewarded with a yawn. Lucy frowned at the page until she was sure she knew the words.

"'There are a whole bunch of actions that will cause a referee to blow her whistle,'" Lucy read out loud. "'Charging, hitting, holding, kicking, pushing, tripping.'" She pulled in her chin. "Good grief, this sounds like Worldwide Wrestling, not soccer!" And there was more. "'Dangerous play. Interfering with the goalkeeper. Un-gentle-man-ly conduct.'" Lucy had an image of butlers hitting each other with trays, but she was pretty sure that wasn't what it meant. In parentheses, it said, "(bad behavior)."

The last word on the list was a hard one. "'Ob-struc-tion.' What does *that* mean, Marmie?"

Lolli answered from under the bed, but it didn't help. Lucy scanned the page and saw the word again in a box in the corner. "Okay, here we go. 'This call means that you've placed your body between your op-po-nent'—that's a player on the other team, like Lolli's your opponent, Marmie—'between your opponent and the ball without going after the ball yourself.' "

Lucy closed her eyes to picture it. Well, yeah, she could see doing that to try to keep a girl on the other team from saving the ball if it was going out of bounds.

She went back to the book. " 'It's not allowed. You can only throw your body in front of another player if you are actually going after the ball.' "

That made sense. Nobody was going to get away with that or any of the other stuff, so why did Rianna and the girls J.J. heard talking even try it?

Of course, Rianna had pulled it on Coach Neely and it had worked.

"That doesn't count," Lucy said to the orange pile in her lap. "Coach Neely doesn't know what's going on half the time. She's either sending a text message or crushing on Seth, whatever that means. I don't care whether Mr. Auggy thinks she's good—she's like a grown-up Mora coaching soccer."

"She won't get away with it in a real game anyway," little Kayla had told Lucy.

But how could she be sure? Kids from big city teams obviously did it.

Lucy searched the page again and jiggled Marmalade awake. "Okay, listen to this: 'There are times when a referee might not call an obvious foul. If a team is about to score, for instance, it wouldn't be fair to stop play and set up a free kick just because the other team fouled.' " Lucy sat up straighter. "Get *this!* 'It might en-cour-age'—okay, yeah, encourage—'It might encourage some players to behave badly and try to foul whenever the other team gets close to the goal.' "

Some players. They might as well have put Rianna's name right in there.

"I just want to go to soccer camp and bounce a ball off of Rianna's head," Lucy said to Marmalade ... and Lollipop, who hopped onto the corner of the bed as if she didn't want to miss this show.

"That's some pretty lively reading going on in there," Dad said from the hallway.

"We're doing great, Dad," Lucy said.

She closed the book and sank onto the pillows again. It was there in writing: nobody got away with ruining the beautiful game. She couldn't wait to tell J.J.

Lucy flew through the house and out the front door, neck already craning toward J.J.'s. Her steps slowed when she saw a white, important-looking car in front of his house.

Nobody ever came to visit the Clucks, except Mr. Auggy and Winnie the State Lady. That wasn't Mr. A's Jeep over there, and it sure looked like something a Child Protective Services person would drive. Lucy sank onto her front step and held out a hand absently to Mudge who joined her, muttering under his cat-breath.

"J.J. didn't say anything about her coming over today," Lucy said to him. "He would've told me."

Or she just would have known. He always got sullen and grumpy when he had to deal with Winnie, even though she was always telling him she was on his side. Even though she'd told J.J. he didn't have to have visits with his father anymore if he didn't want to, J.J. still kept her in the same category as the sheriff and the Easter Bunny: people who weren't to be believed.

But as Lucy fiddled with the hair poking out of Mudge's ears and studied the car, she realized the letters on the side weren't CPS. They were TCPO. She squinted to read what was underneath. Tularosa County Probation Officer.

Probation? Wasn't that kind of like being grounded? Gabe said his dad put him on that when his grades started to slip. Lucy pulled her hand from Mudge's ear. Was J.J. on probation?

Lucy's heart began to pound as if she were the one it had happened to. She was about to go in and grill Dad—he probably knew about this, right?—when the front door opened and a man in a police-looking uniform stepped out. J.J.'s father was with him.

Even from across the street, beyond the fence and half-hidden by the shadows of the cottonwoods, Lucy shrank down in fear. Mr. Cluck was as mean-faced as ever. He was a lot skinnier than he was the last time she'd seen him—sort of like a half-starved junkyard dog—and his eyes were all baggy like he'd had the flu. But the way he walked through the debris in the yard with his fist clenched, as if he were hoping somebody would jump out of an old rusted bathtub and pick a fight with him so he could punch them in the face—that was just as frightening as it had ever been. Lucy's stomach tied into a knot.

"You've got ten minutes," she heard the officer say. "And you can only take what I can fit in my trunk."

Mr. Cluck didn't answer as he bent down, jaw muscles twitching, picked up a rusty hammer, and thrust it into the duffle bag he had swung over his shoulder. Who would want that? Who would want any of that nasty stuff?

"I don't know what you're going to do with that trash," the officer said as if he'd heard Lucy's thoughts.

"It's mine," Mr. Cluck said.

It only took two words for Lucy to want to escape into the house and never come out. His voice sliced into her, just the way it had right there on the corner, the day of their first-ever soccer game last winter when he had come out screaming at J.J. and dragged him away. And exactly as it had that Easter Sunday morning when he had growled at Lucy to get off his property and stay away from his family. She knew the vicious voice had been used in even worse ways on J.J., and that was what terrified her the most.

That, and the way he suddenly got very still and then straightened from the waist to stab his dagger gaze right into her. Lucy gasped out loud.

"What are you lookin' at?" he said.

"Cluck," said the officer, "just take care of your business."

Lucy didn't move. Neither did J.J.'s father. He merely stood with a handful of rusty metal tools, looking as if he wanted to hurl them all at her. And then he smiled.

"Cluck!" the officer said again.

Lucy didn't wait to see what happened after that. She pressed a growling Mudge to her chest and scrambled back into her house. Dad turned off the audio book he was listening to on the Napping Couch and tilted his head.

"What's up, champ?" he said.

"I just saw Evil smile, Dad," she said. "It was the ugliest thing I ever saw."

It took a while to remember that she had something good to tell J.J.—about nobody being able to cheat in soccer. When she did remember, she didn't get to talk to him until they were all headed to the bleachers Monday morning for the big camp assembly. She asked Kayla to save her a seat in their team's section and pulled J.J. to the back of the crowd. Gabe made his usual kissing sound when he saw them, and Lucy felt another stab of homesickness. Things were pretty bad when she was missing *that*.

She took a moment to see if J.J. showed any traces of having talked to his dad, but as soon as Gabe had moved on to harassing Veronica, he just said, "You told Hawke, right?"

"Don't have to."

"Why?"

"Nobody's going to get away with it, J.J."

Lucy told him about what she'd read. His face told her she was clearly nuts.

"These kids don't read books," J.J. said.

"But referees do. I'm telling you, we don't have to worry."

"You think everybody's as honest as you." J.J.'s dark eyes seemed to grow darker. "They aren't." He folded his arms across his chest, leaving a lot of arm still hanging out on either side. "My dad came over yesterday."

"I know."

"I didn't have to talk to him."

"Good."

"He acted weird."

"He always acts weird, J.J."

Lucy didn't mention Mr. Cluck smiling at her and giving her the creeps. Besides, the microphone squealed.

"We gotta go sit with our teams," Lucy said. "We'll talk later, okay?"

"At home."

"No, at lunch."

Before he could argue, Lucy broke away and skittered to the seat Kayla was saving for her. She didn't see Rianna until she leaned over Lucy's shoulder from behind.

"I've been looking all over for you," she said into Lucy's ear.

Why did this girl's breath always feel like it was coming out of Aunt Karen's blow-dryer?

Lucy was glad Hawke started right in, telling the camp how proud he was of all of them and bringing the boys' Select Team onto the field to demonstrate different ways to score goals.

"They get to perform because they're boys," Rianna said to Lucy.

Or because they were some of the best soccer players Lucy had ever seen besides professionals on TV. They did make it look beautiful. Nobody charged or hit or kicked or pushed. They might have been absurd little creeps like Oscar and Gabe off the field, but when they were playing, they were gen-tle-man-ly.

Everybody cheered when the exhibition was over, but Lucy could tell the crowd was getting restless for Hawke to give the VIP award. She thought Rianna was going to chew up somebody's ball cap any minute.

"You've been so focused on your game," Hawke boomed out, "you probably haven't noticed me watching you—all of you."

"I have," Rianna said to Lucy. "I don't miss that much."

"I've seen excellent dribbling, great shooting, awesome goalkeeping—"

"Come on, give the award already," Rianna said.

Lucy scrunched her shoulders.

"But what has impressed me most," Hawke said, "is the good sportsmanship I've observed. The person I am giving this award to today is a team player who cares about the performance of the entire team, who cheers the other players on whether it's in a drill or a practice game—"

Rianna scooted herself to the edge of her seat, so that her knees pressed into Lucy's back. She put a pair of sweaty palms on Lucy's shoulders, and Lucy realized what she was preparing herself for.

"So this week's VIP award goes to a young man you've just seen demonstrate those very qualities—"

"*What?*" Rianna dug her fingers into Lucy's collarbone. "A *boy*. I should have known."

Rianna jerked back onto her seat, and Lucy let out a long breath. Beside her, Kayla gave the tiniest of sniffs.

Well, well.

Rianna didn't have that much to say during morning practice, which made everybody's life easier. Maybe she would pout for the two weeks that were left of camp. Or maybe she'd be mad enough about not getting the award to quit completely.

And maybe the soccer ball would turn into a giant scoop of chocolate ice cream—because when they broke for lunch and Lucy was trying to get her shin guards off so she could go and meet J.J., Rianna elbowed herself right in beside her.

"I have an idea," she said.

"Uh-huh," Lucy said.

"Eat with me, and I'll tell you about it. You're going to want in on it."

"Is it about flopping?" Lucy said.

The words were out before she could catch them, and once they escaped, she was glad. It was the first time she'd seen Rianna surprised.

The startle in her eyes passed quickly, though. "I'm over that," Rianna said. "This is about the award."

Lucy stuffed her shin guards and cleats into her backpack and stuck her foot into one of her tennis shoes.

"Hawke's gonna give it two more times," Rianna said. "You and me deserve it, and I know how we can get it."

By cheating? This time Lucy didn't say it out loud. Her lips were too stunned to move. Was this girl for real?

Rianna stood up. "We can't talk about this here. Let's go over to—"

"I'm already eating lunch with somebody else," Lucy said. She jammed her foot into her other shoe and didn't bother to tie it before she left the bench.

"Are you serious?" Rianna planted herself in front of Lucy. "Don't you get how huge this is?"

"Guess not," Lucy said.

She tried to dodge around Rianna, but she obstructed her. Lucy wished there were referees for conversations.

"If we get VIP awards from this camp, it's like an automatic acceptance into ODP." Rianna put her face close to Lucy's. "There is major competition for that—I'm talking, major. We can't just be great players, which we already are. We have to—"

"I have to meet somebody for lunch," Lucy said.

Rianna slitted her eyes down to dashes. "This is a one-time offer, Rooney. I'm not sharing this idea with anybody else—just you. Don't you get it?"

"No," Lucy said. "I don't."

She used her best shimmy fake and got around Rianna this time. She was two steps away when she felt the grab at her arm.

"Let go," Lucy said.

"Don't think you're gonna tell Coach Neely I have a plan." Rianna squeezed. "I'll know who did it—and I told you, you don't want me for your enemy."

"Actually, I think I do," Lucy said. "Because that would mean I'm not anything like you. Now let go—"

"No—"

"Let her go."

Rianna whipped around, once again in a spasm of surprise.

J.J. stepped forward. His fists were clenched, and his jaw was twitching. Lucy hadn't seen his eyes flash that way in a long time.

He looked like his father.

"It's okay, J.J.," Lucy said.

"Yeah, this is between me and her," Rianna said. "She doesn't need her boyfriend to rescue her."

"Let go," J.J. said. Anger snarled in his voice, and Lucy's stomach tied itself into a knot.

Rianna spit out a laugh. "What are you gonna do about it?"

J.J. took another step forward.

"Don't," Lucy said. She wrenched her arm from Rianna's grasp. "We're done here."

"You just remember what I told you, Rooney," Rianna said.

Lucy turned away and took J.J. with her. When they couldn't hear Rianna breathing like a bull any more, he put his mouth close to her ear.

"I know who that is," he. hissed into it.

"It's Rianna Wallace," Lucy said.

"Whatever—she's the one I heard talking to that other girl. The one who said she'd cheat to 'show Hawke.'"

Lucy stopped and got closer to J.J.'s face, until she could see the tiny beads of sweat under his eyes. "Are you sure?"

"Yeah. She has that spitty laugh. What did she tell you?"

"That you were right," Lucy said. "Everybody isn't honest." She shook her head. "But J.J., you can't get in trouble over this, okay? You can't."

She looked back over her shoulder. Rianna was gone, but the knot in Lucy's stomach was very much still there. The same knot she'd felt yesterday when she saw Mr. Cluck.

Somebody had to do something. She just wished it didn't have to be her.

10

When Dusty's mom pulled up at Lucy's side gate that afternoon to drop her off, Dad's assistant, Luke, was letting him out too.

"Isn't your father home early?" Mrs. Terricola said.

Carla Rosa gave an I-have-bad-news nod. "Guess what? My dad only comes home early when he's had a bad day. Really bad."

"It's only a bad day when my dad *does* come home," Januarie said.

"Thanks," Lucy said as she climbed out of the SUV. Her stomach was still in that knot, and nothing they were saying was making her feel better.

"Come over later if you can, *Bolillo*," Dusty said through the window. "We can watch a DVD or something. I miss you."

Lucy nodded. She'd love to go over to Dusty's and pretend she was just a normal kid whose worst problem was deciding what movie to watch, but the slump of Dad's back told her even *Monsters, Inc.* wouldn't do it. There was no sunshine in the smile he tried to arrange on his face.

"Hey, Champ," he said when she slid under his arm inside the gate.

"Are you sick?" she said.

"Do I look sick?"

"Kind of. Not like you have the flu sick. Worried sick."

Dad attempted a chuckle and waved in the direction of the patio table. "I guess that's where that expression comes from. Sit with me, Luce."

It was hot enough to cook pancakes on the cement, but Lucy parked herself in a chair under the umbrella and felt her stomach go into a square knot. The only reason to talk out here instead of inside under the ceiling fan was so Inez and Mora wouldn't hear. That couldn't be good.

Dad took a long time getting situated in his chair with his legs folded just so before he finally said, "Did you listen to me on the radio the day of the storm?"

"Until the power went off," Lucy said.

"How was I? Honestly."

Lucy rewound the memories. So much had happened since then, it seemed like two birthdays must have passed. All she could remember was that he didn't sound like molasses pouring.

"Different?" Dad said.

"Yeah. Like maybe there were so many things going on you couldn't—I mean, there *was* a storm—and, like, everything was confusing."

"Exactly." Dad rubbed his whole face with his hand like he was washing it off. "Luke wasn't there, so I was on my own."

"Then you did good!" Lucy said.

"For a man who can't see."

"Right."

"And that isn't good enough."

Lucy got up on one knee. "Who says?"

"The new people who just bought our station."

"I don't get it," Lucy said.

But actually she did. What Dad was about to say crept up on her like a snake. She knew it was going to bite her.

"Did you get fired?" she said.

Dad's eyes darted until they found someplace close to hers. "Not yet," he said.

"Are you *going* to get fired?"

"Maybe."

"Dad, that's not fair!" Lucy's voice wound up to the top of the umbrella. "You're the best! You can't help it if you can't see!"

"And neither can they, Luce."

Dad stretched his hand across the table. She was in no mood to be calmed down, but she stuck hers under it anyway. She was sure he could feel it going stiff as a chicken claw.

"Here's the deal," he said. "The old owners were fine with Luke always being there to help me. They probably wouldn't even have minded what happened during the storm. But things have changed—"

"This is what you told me to be ready for," Lucy said. And she wasn't. Not even close.

"The new owners have given me three choices," Dad said. "I can improve my technical skills so I can handle my broadcasts on my own, if necessary, or I can transfer to another station where I'll be part of a larger team, although I won't have my own show like I do here. Or—"

"Or you can get fired," Lucy said.

Dad nodded.

"So really you only have two choices."

He nodded again.

Something tickled at the back of Lucy's brain. "Where's the other station that you would be transferred to?"

Dad cleared his throat. "El Paso."

"No way! Aunt Karen will never leave me alone then!"

"I didn't think you'd be too crazy about that idea. But I'm not sure you're going to like the other one any better."

Lucy sank back on her foot. "About you learning new technical stuff? Why?"

"It means I'll have to go to a school in Albuquerque—a special school for the blind—and stay there for six weeks."

"I'd go with you, right? Since it's summer."

Dad gave her hand a squeeze. "The next class doesn't start until the end of August, just when you start school again."

"Then what—?" Lucy closed her eyes, but everything looked just as confused behind them.

"You would stay here. With someone, of course." Dad tried the smile again. "Not that I don't think you could make it by yourself. You run this place anyway, but Sheriff Navarro would have me thrown in jail. Then we'd really be in trouble."

They were already in the biggest mess Lucy could think of. What kind of choice was this? Leave her friends and her team—which she already knew from soccer camp was like having a stomach virus that never ended—*and* be around Aunt Karen all the time, or stay here, away from Dad, with some babysitter.

"Could Inez live with me?" she said. "That could work, couldn't it?"

"I'm sure she'll do what she's doing for us now, but she has her farm and Mora to take care of. I can't ask her to rearrange all of that."

"Then who?"

"I don't know, Luce. I'm still praying about it. In the meantime, I just want you to keep being the best Lucy you can be, okay? And pray—will you?"

Lucy nodded.

"I hope that's a yes," Dad said.

"It is," Lucy said.

"We'll get the right answer."

Dad didn't add that everything was going to turn out perfectly. They both knew that wasn't how God worked. If it was, Mom would be here and Dad would be able to see and the three of them would be firing up a grill to cook hot dogs instead of having this conversation.

"We'll get through it, champ," Dad said. "Now—tell me about your day." He made the sandpaper chuckle work this time. "I bet it was better than mine."

Not much. In fact, it was too bad to talk about right now.

"I learned how to do a diving header off a corner kick," she said instead.

"Is that good?" Dad said.

"Oh, yeah," Lucy said. At least something was.

Tuesday morning, Dusty was in the very back seat of Veronica's van when they picked up Lucy for camp, and she motioned for Lucy to join her. Veronica was in the front seat, making a huge deal out of not speaking to her mother, and Carla Rosa was in the second seat, "guess whatting" Januarie about something. It didn't seem to matter to her that Januarie was fiddling with the contents of her backpack and showing no signs of listening at all.

"How come you didn't come over yesterday, *Bolillo?*" Dusty whispered as Lucy buckled her seatbelt beside her.

"I couldn't."

"Did you get in trouble or something?"

Lucy shook her head and pretended that seatbelt fastening was way more complicated than it was. After Dad's news about the radio station, she'd forgotten all about Dusty's invitation. She'd practically forgotten everything, except to pray in her Book of Lists—although unless God made some kind of miracle happen, she didn't see how all the begging and whining she'd written down was going to do any good.

"You know something, Lucy?"

Lucy looked up sharply at the tone of Dusty's voice. It sounded like tears weren't far away.

They weren't. They were about to spill over onto Dusty's cheeks.

Lucy didn't know what to do. She'd only recently figured out what to do when *she* cried.

She decided on, "What?"

Dusty blinked fast. "I know you can't eat lunch with us, but I don't think your coach said you can't talk to us *any* time."

"She never—"

Dusty curled her fingers around Lucy's T-shirt and pulled her in closer—as if Lucy weren't practically sitting in her lap already.

"I wanted you to come over because I can't talk to anybody else about this—"

"About—?"

"And it might not be happening if you didn't have to be on that other team—even though I know it's the special team and you deserve that—but without you, everything is so awful—"

"What—?"

"Veronica's grounded because my mom told her mom she saw her holding hands with the new boy on our team—"

"What new—?"

"So she won't talk to me *or* her mom—like it was *my* fault my mom can't mind her own business—although, I was already mad at Veronica because she's so busy flirting with Zen—"

"Who in the world—?"

"—she doesn't pay any attention to soccer—which doesn't actually matter because neither does Seth, and he's supposed to be the coach but all he does is send text messages and say we have to work out our own problems, which we wouldn't even have if you were there." Dusty took a breath and surged on. "Gabe is all mad because he isn't on the Boys' Select Team, so he's in a bad mood all the time—plus now Veronica likes Zen—"

"Who—?"

"—and even though Gabe pretends he doesn't like Veronica as a girlfriend, he likes it that *she* likes *him*—so anyway he's being stupid like he used to be, all acting like a moron, and I tried to talk to Mr. Auggy, and he said we need to talk to our own coach but Seth—"

"—is too busy sending text messages to *my* coach," Lucy managed to get in.

"Yes!" Dusty's eyes filled with new tears. "I knew you'd get it!"

Lucy didn't, but she nodded anyway.

"Soccer used to be so fun," Dusty said, "and now I don't even like it anymore. I wish we could just stay in Los Suenos and play on our own field—only we don't even have one now. We're not the Dreams—we're the Nightmares!"

All Lucy could do was nod, but that seemed to give Dusty permission to let go of all the crying she'd been holding back. She pasted her face to Lucy's shoulder and sobbed.

"Everything all right back there?" Veronica's mother said.

"Guess what?" Carla Rosa said. "I think Dusty's crying."

"Tell them I'm fine," Dusty whispered to Lucy.

"You're not," Lucy whispered back.

"Dusty?" Mrs. DeMatteo said. "Veronica, did you hurt Dusty's feelings?"

"Why is it always my fault?"

"Because you are a drama queen—"

While Veronica and her mother batted that back and forth and Carla Rosa and Januarie looked on like they were watching a TV show, Dusty lifted her face and gave Lucy a watery smile.

"I *am* fine now," she said. "I'm glad we finally talked."

We hadn't, and Lucy had more questions than she had answers. What was happening to her Los Suenos Dreams? Why *had* soccer turned into a nightmare?

And who in the world was Zen?

Mrs. DeMatteo stopped the van in the parking lot, and the doors flew open. Veronica flounced out of the front seat, and Januarie shot from the second seat like Godzilla was after her.

"Guess what?" Carla Rosa said.

"What?" Lucy and Dusty said together. Dusty giggled.

"Januarie has something she's not supposed to have."

Lucy sighed. "What is it?"

Carla Rosa shrugged. "I don't know."

"Then how do you—"

"I can just tell. Guess what—she can't get in trouble or those foster care people will take her—"

Dusty squeezed Lucy's arm. "Don't worry. I'll tell J.J."

She ran off happily with Carla Rosa, leaving Lucy feeling like her head was on backward.

The instant Lucy sat on the bench to put on her cleats, Rianna appeared beside her as if somebody had beamed her down from a spaceship. Lucy concentrated on her shoelaces to keep herself from shoving her off the end. There just wasn't room for her bullying right now.

But Rianna's voice was high and light as she said, "For you, Rooney," and put a piece of blue paper in Lucy's lap. "Here's one for you, Sarah—Kayla—"

Rianna handed out a whole stack of blue papers as if she were distributing Halloween candy. Lucy forced herself to look at hers. It was probably guidelines for flopping and charging and obstructing.

Lucy felt her eyes bug, though, as she read the words typed at the top in bold red letters: FAIR PLAY CODE.

Was she kidding?

* Play fair.

* Play to win, but accept defeat with dignity.

* Observe the laws of the game.

* Denounce those who attempt to discredit our sport.

Lucy blinked. She wasn't even sure what that one meant, but it didn't sound like something Rianna believed. Neither did the last item.

* Use soccer to make a better world.

"You wrote this?" Sarah said. She looked as if she sincerely doubted it.

Coach Neely looked up from her copy. "It's the FIFA Fair Play Code."

"Didn't I put that on there somewhere?" Rianna said.

Lucy looked. She hadn't. She'd made it look like she made it up herself.

"What's FIFA?" Waverly said, not smiling, as usual.

"Excuse me for being a moron," Patricia muttered.

"This is great, Rianna," Coach Neely said, but she looked a little uncomfortable, like she had a piece of meat between her back molars. "Do you have permission to hand this out though? Hawke has to okay any flyers—"

"Oh, yeah." Rianna straightened importantly. "I had a lo-o-ong talk with him yesterday because—" She looked around, like there might be spies in the group.

"Because what?" Coach Neely said. "You can trust your team."

Lucy chomped down on her lip.

"Okay, well." Rianna tossed her ponytail. "I went to him because I found out that some people—on other teams, not ours—aren't playing by the rules. They're, like, playing dirty and then saying it's only cheating if you get caught."

Lucy knew her mouth had fallen open, but she couldn't close it.

"I told him I didn't want our camp to be like that," Rianna went on. "And I asked him if I could hand out a flyer."

"You made this yourself?" Coach Neely said. She took off her sunglasses. She was clearly impressed.

"Oh yeah. It's not that hard with a computer. And I was really into it."

"We should all be into it." Coach Neely gave Rianna one more admiring look before she put her sunglasses back on. "Rianna's set an example for us—what do you say we set one for the rest of the teams?"

Taylor snorted. Patricia muttered something. Everyone else looked at Lucy, for no reason she could figure out. But the only face she could look back at was Rianna's. She sent Lucy an eye-message so clear she might as well have yelled it across the soccer field.

I bet you wish you listened to me. Now I'm getting all the credit.

Lucy turned and squinted into the sun, just so she wouldn't send back: *I am SO going to tell EVERYBODY that this is just a way for you to get the VIP award—and you don't deserve it!*

It was so hard not to. Maybe she even would have—if familiar movement hadn't caught her eye on the other side of the field, where the Los Suenos Dreams were kicking the ball around a line of orange cones. J.J. was dribbling like that mad dog Mr. Auggy was always talking about—and Gabe was sticking his foot in like a stick in a bicycle spoke instead of dribbling his own ball. Carla Rosa looked like Lucy had never worked with her for a single minute, much less hours in her backyard. Oscar and Emanuel were doing nothing but punching each other, and she could hear Veronica squealing as a tall, fast kid with a lot of hair stole her ball.

Lucy would have called it a nightmare—that is, if Dusty hadn't waved her arms over her head and gathered everyone around her, and they hadn't all looked like they were listening. Like they wanted the Dreams to come back.

"Well, what about it?" Coach Neely said.

Lucy pulled her eyes away from her friends. "I say we go for it," she said. "Play clean and fair." She waved the blue sheet. "Just like this says."

She looked straight at Rianna, who had the nerve to look right back. Her eyes weren't friendly.

Late that afternoon, Lucy and J.J. and Januarie went to Pasco's café for grilled cheese sandwiches. Inez had to take Mora to dance class, and Dad said Lucy could treat J.J. and Januarie to an early supper, like they used to do before Inez became Lucy's nanny. He even called Felix and told him to put whatever they wanted on his account.

Lucy waited until Januarie was busy picking out a flavor from the ice cream case—a major decision-making process apparently—before she said, "Rianna still acts like one of those little terrier dogs the way she bosses us all around. But when we were playing our practice game today, she didn't try to get me to fall down, and she didn't pull on anybody's shirt or foul on purpose."

She chewed on the extra pickle Felix put on her plate, "For old time's sake," he'd told her, with that sad look he had in his eyes these days.

"Maybe she won't try to cheat now," Lucy went on. "Maybe she'll just get noticed being, like, the Fair Play Queen instead of scoring goals any dirty way she can. She could 'show' Hawke whatever she wants to show him that way."

"You believe that?" J.J said.

Lucy shrugged. "I want to. Don't you?"

J.J. didn't answer.

"Don't you just want to get back to playing soccer?" she said.

He still didn't answer.

"You can't be so negative all the time, J.J."

He didn't seem to hear her. He had his neck craned toward the ice cream case.

"You want dessert?" Lucy said. "You didn't even eat your sandwich yet."

"Januarie," he said.

"What about her?"

"What's she doing?"

Lucy squinted. "Trying to decide between mint chocolate chip and that gross thing with the marshmallows—and I'm not getting her two scoops."

J.J. shook his head and pointed. When Lucy looked even closer, she saw that Januarie wasn't checking out the ice cream at all. She was loading her pockets with ketchup packets from the basket on Felix's counter.

"What's up with that?" Lucy said.

"She's weird."

"At least she's not bugging us all the time." Lucy nudged him. "Now that she has her own team, you don't have to be her babysitter every minute."

J.J. grunted.

"What?" Sometimes she really did wish he would use more actual words.

"She's started cussing."

"Nuh-uh!"

"The girls on her team do it."

"They're in fourth grade!"

Lucy knew she was overdoing the exclamation points, but this discussion screamed for them. J.J. shrugged.

"I haven't been helping you with her," Lucy said. "Maybe that's why."

"Mustard," J.J. said.

"Huh?"

He pointed to the counter. "Now she's getting mustard."

Januarie was indeed stuffing yellow plastic packets into the back pockets of her shorts.

"She looks like she's growing an extra—"

"Don't say it, J.J." Lucy put her hand over her mouth, but a large guffaw splattered out anyway.

"How many condiments do you need for ice cream?" Felix Pasco leaned on his glass counter between the stack of menus and the jar where people put their tips.

"Busted," J.J. muttered.

"What are condiments?" Januarie said.

"All that mustard and ketchup you just took." Felix shook his square head, but he still looked more sad than mad as far as Lucy could tell. "You would be welcome to all that I have. *Mi casa es su casa.*"

"Huh?" Januarie said.

Felix just moaned on. "But now I have to watch every penny. Times are hard, *muchacha.*"

Lucy remembered where she'd heard that before. Dad and Mr. Auggy told her that when she got so angry about the big corporation that was trying to bribe people like Felix out of their votes against the soccer field.

"He's not gonna bust her if that's what you're worried about."

Lucy looked at J.J. in surprise. He was watching her and speaking without even moving his lips.

"That's not what I'm worried about," she mumbled back.

She jerked her head toward the door, and they both slipped out while Felix was still lecturing Januarie about the economy. Lucy was sure Januarie didn't know what that was either.

"Let's go to our soccer field," she said.

"Sheriff said not to," J.J. said, even as he took two long-legged strides toward Highway 54.

"That was right after the flood. I think it's okay now."

"Race ya, then."

They ran almost the whole way, and Lucy guessed they'd gotten to the tumble-down bleachers before Januarie even knew they'd left the cafe. She would probably talk Felix into two scoops after all. Lucy leaned over to catch her breath.

"Why'd you want to come here?" J.J. said.

"I don't know." Actually she did, but she wasn't quite sure even J.J. would understand that she just wanted to let the field know somebody still cared about it.

"I liked playin' here." J.J. 's voice squeaked on the 'here.' "Better than camp."

Lucy nodded. Maybe it wasn't as slick as High Noon, but it was their place — their safe place.

"You cryin'?" J.J. said.

"Hello! No!" Lucy smeared at her eyes with the heels of her hands and turned her face to the refreshment stand. Someone had taken all the fallen-down parts and put them in a pile, leaving the building where their fans had once bought Felix's nachos and Claudia's chocolate soccer balls looking naked and embarrassed. The splintered lumber from the bleachers was also in a neat stack, which made it easier to see that the metal frame that had once held them together was still standing as if it were waiting to be covered in seats once more.

Lucy went to it and ran her hand along the metal. She might even have told it she would make sure it got fixed, right out loud, if J.J. hadn't been there. And if her hand hadn't caught on a sharp edge.

"Yikes!" she said as she drew it back. Blood beaded from her palm and trickled toward her wrist. She stuck it up to her mouth.

"What?" J.J. said.

"I cut myself."

"Bad?"

"Nah."

Lucy took another look at her hand and pressed down on it with her other thumb. She hadn't been a tomboy all her life without seeing a little blood once in awhile. J.J., meanwhile, examined the metal.

"Wind didn't do it," he said.

"Huh?"

Lucy forgot her hand and leaned in to look. The metal was cut and bent, and not just there but further down, and on the next support, too. With a chill, she remembered Dad and Mr. Auggy talking again. *I'm thinking something more than the storm hit it,* Mr. Auggy had said.

"Did it get hit with something?" Lucy said to J.J.

J.J. didn't answer. He was walking over to the stack of ruined wood, and when he got there, he kicked at it, knocking it over. He pawed through it with his foot.

"What are you looking for?' Lucy said, though she had a feeling she already knew. "Is it that tire thing we found before? You think somebody used that to tear up what the wind left? "

J.J. still didn't answer. He just kept shoving wood around, first with his feet and then with his hands, until the way he was throwing it started to scare Lucy.

"I don't think it's here," she said, She swallowed hard. "Maybe we shouldn't be either."

J.J. pulled back his arm and hurled a short, smashed board so hard it slid a long time on the dusty ground and set up an anxious swirl of dirt around it. Lucy could taste it on her dry tongue.

"Come on, J.J,," she said. "I don't want to be here. "

Finally he grunted and followed Lucy back to the road. They trudged along saying nothing until Lucy couldn't stand it any longer.

"You know what I bet?" she said. "I bet it was those evil people that want to build the mini-market. I bet they came after the storm and smashed it all up so we'd all think the wind did it."

"It wasn't them," J.J. said.

Lucy stopped in the middle of the bridge over the creek and stared at his back as he kept going.

"How do you know?" she said.

"I just do," he said.

Without looking back at her he waved his arm for her to come on. She hurried to catch up, but she already knew this conversation, too, was over.

It seemed like nothing ever got where it needed to go any more.

11

"Ready for a little Knockout, ladies?" Coach Neely said Wednesday morning.

"That depends on who gets knocked out," Waverly said. She surprised Lucy with a smile.

"You don't know that game?" Rianna looked at Coach Neely—probably to make sure she was still impressed with her. "It's where you find, like, a wall, and mark off a goal area, only we'd have to do it with cones, and then—"

Coach Neely threw her arm around Rianna's neck. "Sorry, Rianna, but we're going to use a real goal and a real goalie. Who wants to volunteer to play goalkeeper first?"

Rianna only looked miffed for a second. Then she said, "I'll do it" like she was offering the team a huge favor.

"Oh, brother," Patricia muttered to Lucy.

On the other side of her, Taylor gave Lucy her snort.

"Line up, team," Coach Neely called out. "The first person takes a shot at the goal. If Rianna blocks it—"

"Which I will," Rianna put in.

"The next person has to get the rebound and try to one-touch it into the goal, and so on. Got it?"

"Huh?" Sarah said.

"Yeah, we've got it," Rianna said.

Coach Neely blew her whistle.

Kayla gave Lucy a tiny push. "You go first. She's not gonna try anything with *you*."

Lucy was sure Rianna wasn't going to try anything at all, not now that she'd made such a big deal out of Fair Play. Lucy even smiled at her as she studied her position. Rianna was already on one knee, as if she knew Lucy was going to send in a ground ball. Lucy ran up on the ball and lobbed it into the air over Rianna's head. It bounced cheerfully into the goal.

"Heads-up, Rianna!" Coach Neely said. "You showed your opponent what you were expecting her to do."

"I know," Rianna said through tight teeth and kicked the ball—hard—toward the line of players.

So much for Fair Play.

Rianna didn't allow another ball to get past her, and by the time it was Lucy's turn again, Lucy could tell she was getting tired.

"You want me to be goalie now?" Lucy said to Coach Neely.

"What?" Rianna said. "No, try to score on me, Rooney."

"Remember, this is about practicing rebounds," Coach Neely said.

Lucy dribbled the ball away from the goal, passed it to Bella, and let Bella pass it back to her. She could feel Rianna watching her, trying to guess what she was going to do. She stood in the middle of the goal, slightly crouched, looking ready for anything. She really was a great soccer player. If only they could work *together*.

"Shoot it already!" Rianna yelled at her and stood straight up.

Up. Tall.

Lucy didn't take the time to set up her shot. She sent a ground ball along the edge of the goal. Rianna had to dive for it and just missed snagging it before it slid into the back corner. Behind Lucy, the team cheered like they were competing in the Euro Cup. Rianna scrambled up, face twisted into a red knot.

"That's not fair! There aren't any defenders! You can't expect me to do this all by myself!"

"Rianna, it's not about that." Coach Neely came toward them, sunglasses on top of her head. "I said we're just practicing rebounds."

"Make *her* be goalie then." Rianna jabbed a finger toward Lucy.

But Coach Neely shook her head. "I think I'll be goalie. That will be fair to everybody."

"We're all about Fair Play, right?" Sarah said to Rianna as she punched herself into the line.

"Whatever," Rianna said, and sent Lucy a look that slithered through her like a worm.

At lunch, Lucy let out a long, relieved breath when she saw Rianna head away from their table.

"What is *with* her?" Sarah said, flipping her very long ponytail over her shoulder.

Taylor's black eyes narrowed. "We had a girl like her on our team at home. She was totally bossy. We were so glad to see her go."

"What happened to her?" little Kayla said.

"We killed her."

"What?"

"No you did *not!*"

"Nuh–*uh!*"

"Just kidding!" Taylor smiled so big she showed every one of her too-many teeth. "But trust me, we wanted to at least put her down the garbage disposal."

Patricia pushed her out–of–control hair back tighter into her headband and pointed at Lucy. "What do you think we should do about her?"

"Me?" Lucy said.

"We can't just let her ruin our whole team." Patricia looked around the table. "Right?"

Only Bella shook her head.

"What?" Sarah said to her.

Bella held up one of Rianna's blue fliers.

"What?" Taylor said.

Bella just looked at Lucy. Everybody did.

"The Fair Play Code," Lucy said.

Taylor snorted. "Which Rianna totally doesn't believe in. She's up to something."

Lucy studied the peanut butter and pickle sandwich Dad had packed for her.

Patricia squinted at her. "You know something, don't you?"

"EWWWWWW!"

All heads snapped to the far end of the picnic area, where it looked like the junior girls' team had just shaken all the members out of their seats. Even from six tables away, Lucy could hear them squawking—

"Gro-oss!"

"Nasty!"

"Oh, no, you did *not!*"

Laughter laced the voices, all except one. A chubby child, even plumper than Januarie, stood in the midst of the squealers, twisting as if she were trying, unsuccessfully, to see her own backside. As the other girls pointed and gasped and howled, she opened her mouth and squalled, "I didn't poop my pants! You put mustard in my chair! *You—*"

She navigated her chunky self around and thrust a finger straight at Januarie.

Lucy didn't know which to stare at: the runny yellow mess plastered all over the back of the poor kid's shorts or the red, delighted face of J.J.'s little sister. Lucy had never seen her look that pleased with herself.

"That is so immature," Waverly said.

Sarah shook her head. "It's the way some kids are raised."

"And where they're from," Taylor said. "That one girl is just trash. And that other one's sister is the girl that got kicked out the very first day."

Lucy stood up. By now, Mustard Girl was sobbing, and no one on her team had even handed her a Kleenex. Januarie was doubled over with laughter.

"Are you through eating already?" Sarah said.

Lucy didn't answer. She just marched past the tables where most kids had gone back to their sandwiches and juice boxes and stopped behind the crying girl.

"Who has a napkin?" Lucy said.

"She needs toilet paper!" somebody said, and the giggling reached a new height.

"Hey! Napkin! Now!"

Nine-year-old bodies froze. A very skinny one snatched up a wet wipe and tossed it to Lucy.

"Hold still," Lucy said to the mustard-drenched girl who was now hiccupping so hard Lucy thought her teeth might rattle out. She went after the back of her shorts with the wet wipe, but she spat her words at the figure who stood there like she'd been shot and hadn't quite been able to fall down.

"Apologize, Januarie," Lucy said.

"It wasn't my idea," Januarie said. "They—"

"I'm not talking to them—I'm talking to *you*. Apologize."

"She can't make you, Jan-Jan," somebody said.

Lucy glared at her. Januarie mumbled something that sounded like it might be, "I'm sorry" and took a step back.

Right into a pair of long legs.

"Do we have a problem here?" Hawke said.

All the little mouths that had had so much to say moments before were suddenly silent. Fingernails, shoelaces, and belly buttons became instantly interesting. Hawke looked at Lucy, but she wasn't sure what to say either.

"Lucy?" he said. "Problem?"

"An accident with some mustard, sir," Lucy said.

Hawke searched them all with his eyes, picking them clean. Lucy thought she heard at least one girl sniff. They were all sweating; she was sure of that.

"I hope whoever was careless has apologized," he said finally.

"We're working on it," Lucy said.

He looked down at Mustard Girl and tilted his head. "Are you satisfied with that, Yo-Yo?"

There was one big holding of breath. Januarie's face was almost blue.

Slowly, "Yo-Yo" nodded.

"Then let's go find your coach and see if we can come up with some clean clothes for you to change into." Hawke looked over his shoulder at Lucy. "I'd like to talk to you later," he said.

When he was gone, Januarie's team melted into a blob at Lucy's feet.

"Thank you SO much—"

"We would have gotten in so much trouble—"

"You're not gonna tell on us now are you?"

Lucy held up her hand, but they kept begging until Januarie said, "You better listen."

"You guys should have thought about all that before you put mustard on that girl's seat," Lucy said. "Didn't you get the Fair Play Code this morning? The blue sheet?"

"I thought that was about soccer," the very skinny girl said.

"It's about acting like a human." Lucy gave them all a black look. "I'm not helping you next time—so don't let there be a next time."

Heads bobbed. Eyes filled. Mouths let out sighs. Lucy was sure they'd all head for the bathroom as soon as she walked away.

She didn't get two steps before Januarie was tugging at her hand.

"Are you gonna tell, really?" she said.

"I should."

"But *are* you? You can't, Lucy, or my whole team will hate me."

Lucy stopped and shook away Januarie's hand. "What were you thinking doing that to that girl, Januarie? Don't you hate it when kids tease you?"

"Yeah, but—"

"Then I don't get it."

"They dared me to do it because her sister's that girl that yelled at the ref, and everybody hates her, and I had to—"

"What?"

"They just started being friends with me. If I didn't, they wouldn't like me."

"If they can't like you just because you're you, they aren't your friends anyway." Lucy's words rang in her own head, as if she'd just said them to herself. She looked over at her own table, where half the team looked quickly away, and the other half was already whispering to each other.

It's where they're from, they'd all agreed.

If they find out you're from Los Suenos, they'll make fun of you, J.J. had warned her.

Lucy turned to leave Januarie there alone, but she grabbed at Lucy's wrist again.

"Are you gonna tell J.J.?" she said.

"I don't know."

"Please don't!"

"I said I don't know!"

Before they could exchange any more exclamation points, Lucy pulled away. Lunch was over. She picked up her lunch bag and went back to the soccer field.

"I hear you're wiping noses now," Rianna whispered to Lucy when Coach Neely was dividing them up for the afternoon match.

Lucy leaned over to stretch. Rianna went down with her.

"While you were doing lunch duty, *I* was talking to Hawke about the ODP people." Rianna shook her head. "Too bad. You could have been in on it too, if you weren't busy hanging out with losers."

She popped back up before Lucy could tell her she'd just caught her in a big fat lie. And she said *Lucy* was a loser.

Lucy was barely buckled into the van before Dusty poked a folded piece of paper into her hand. She drummed her fingers while Lucy read it.

> Something is WAY wrong with J.J.
> He won't talk to anybody. Help!!!!

Lucy opened her mouth, but Dusty put a finger to her lips and darted her eyes toward Januarie. Lucy didn't tell her they didn't need to worry about Januarie being a little snitch right now. She figured she could tell Januarie she'd won the lottery and she wouldn't breathe a word to anybody.

Instead, Lucy took the purple pen Dusty handed her and scribbled, "I'll find out."

But when Veronica's mom dropped them off, J.J. was already at his front door, and Lucy watched him disappear inside.

"Did you decide?" Januarie's voice wound up into Chihuahua range. "Are you gonna tell J.J. on me?"

Lucy held out her hand. "Give me all the mustard and ketchup you have. All of it."

Januarie dumped her whole backpack onto the brick sidewalk. There must have been ten packets mixed in with her cleats and shin guards and candy bars.

"I won't tell him," Lucy said when Januarie had handed over the condiments, "if you promise me you will—"

"I'll never play a trick on Yo-Yo again. I swear. Even if she does have the weirdest name ever."

"Not good enough," Lucy said. "You have to promise to make friends with her."

Januarie's double ponytails nearly stood straight up. "Friends?" she said.

"Am I speaking French? Yes, friends. Do you promise?"

Januarie looked as if Lucy was requiring her to fork over all the candy bars too.

"You're mean, Lucy," she said, lower lip wobbling.

"So are you, Januarie," Lucy said, "and I am so sick of mean people."

12

Lucy slammed her way through every gate and door until she was in the kitchen. Mora even looked up from her cell phone.

"Who peed in your Cheerios?" she said.

Inez hissed at her and rested a soft gaze on Lucy.

"You are *colerico,* Senorita?" she said.

"That's angry—"

"Yes!"

Lucy dropped into her chair and glared at the tortilla chips in the wooden bowl. They were Inez's homemade ones, still steaming, but Lucy pushed them away.

"Wow." Mora set her phone aside and practically licked her chops. "Is it about a boy?"

"It's about people being stupid and bossy."

"Oh, I hate that," Mora said. She scooted her chair in. "So, dish. I want details."

"I think we will look to Senora Queen Esther instead," Inez said.

"No offense, Inez," Lucy said, "but I don't see how she's gonna help me this time. I'm not a queen."

"You have the same power," Inez said. "You will see."

Mora rolled her eyes and selected a chip. Lucy sighed.

After Inez ran a brown finger down the tissue paper page with her lips moving silently, she closed her eyes as if she was seeing the story behind her eyelids.

"There is one evil *hombre* in the court of Senor King," she said.

"There always is," Mora said. "Otherwise there wouldn't be a story."

"His name is Senor Haman, and he is the highest next to Senor King." Inez's eyes darkened. "But he is hungry for the power, and he makes the law that every person must bow down to him."

Mora stopped in mid-bite. "I wouldn't bow down to him."

Lucy was sure Mora wouldn't. She couldn't even picture it.

"Everyone, they bow down to Senor Haman, but not Senor Mordecai. He is the Jew. He will bow to no one but God. Senor Haman wants to kill Senor Mordecai, and not only him, but all the Jewish people."

"See?" Lucy said. "People are just mean."

"Senor King, he trusts Senor Haman. He says okay kill the Jews, and they must not fight back."

"What did they ever do to him?" Mora said.

Inez folded her hands. "They worship God, not him."

"Well, yeah, God is, like, *God!*"

"Senor King—he does not believe this. Senor Haman, he says Senor King will lose his power if the Jews, they are not killed—"

"Wait a minute," Lucy said. "That means all Esther's relatives will get killed."

"But not her," Mora said. "King Hottie doesn't know she's a Jew. I hope she keeps her mouth shut."

Inez went back to the open Bible. "Senora Queen Esther, she does not know of this plan of Senor Haman. She only hear her people weeping in the street. She can see Senor Mordecai at the gate, dress in the sackcloth and the ashes."

Mora wrinkled her nose. "Gross. What's that about?"

"This is what the Jew will do when he mourns. So everyone, they will know his grief."

"But Esther doesn't know why he's all crying and stuff," Lucy said.

"No, until Senor Mordecai send the messenger to Senora Queen. He tells her, go to Senor King and ask for the mercy for the Jewish people."

"But she can't!" Mora cried. "He'll find out she's a Jew too!"

"That is not the most worser," Inez said.

Lucy didn't see how it could get any 'worser.'

"If Senora Queen Esther go to the king when he has not called for her, she could be put to the death."

"What?" Mora said. "That is just wrong!"

"But it is so," Inez said. She looked from Mora to Lucy and back again, her black eyes shining. "What will you do if this is you?"

Mora opened her mouth, but to Lucy's surprise, she looked at her.

"What do we do, Lucy?" she said.

"Why are you asking me?"

"Because you always know the right thing to do. You're like one of these people—" She wafted a hand toward the Bible. "Only your name's not as weird as theirs."

Lucy stared at her.

"Well, you *are*," Mora said. "I bet you'd go marching in there to King Hottie and tell him to back off your people. You totally would."

"That is what Senora Queen Esther, she does," Inez said in a quiet voice.

Mora put her hands over her ears. "If the king kills her, I don't want to hear it."

"He does, doesn't he?" Lucy said to Inez. "The story can't end that way!"

"In case you haven't noticed," Mora said, pulling her hands from her head, "this isn't Disney we're studying." She stuck her hands back over her ears. "Tell me when she's done with the bad part."

"I think we stop here for today," Inez said.

"Abuela!" Mora wailed. "I hate it when you do that." She pushed her chair away from the table. "Is there any more salsa?"

She went to the refrigerator, and Inez put her warm, brown hand on Lucy's.

"Senora Queen Esther, she will help you."

Lucy shook her head. "I don't know how."

"You will," Inez said. "You will."

Lucy settled in that night to read to Marmalade—and Lolli, who joined them on the bed and pretended to be more interested in bathing than in goalkeeping. But Lucy couldn't read more than a paragraph without crawling to the window to see if there was a signal from J.J. He hadn't answered any of the signals she'd tried to send him.

"You know what?" she said to the kitties. "J.J.'s acting like Mortimer—no, Mordecai—whatever they call him." Mora was right about the names. "Dusty says J.J.'s all moping and weird. I just wish he'd send over a messenger."

She sighed. They used to use Januarie for that. It seemed like everything had changed. And she wanted it all back the way it was before—even some of the things they thought were so bad. This was much worse.

There was a tap on the door.

"Yes, I'm reading," Lucy said.

Dad popped his head in. "I wasn't checking up on you. I just knew you'd want to know that Aunt Karen called." Even though they were sightless, his eyes could still sparkle.

Lucy stiffened. "She's not back from her vacation, is she?"

Dad chuckled. "You still have another week, Luce. She actually sounded like she was having fun."

"Uh-huh," Lucy said. Aunt Karen's idea of fun was having her nails done.

"I think this trip has been good for her." He grinned. "And for us."

Lucy loved Dad for saying that. He really was the best at understanding stuff. She sat up straighter. Why hadn't she told him all about the soccer tangle? And about what they suspected about the soccer field?

"And Champ?"

"Yeah, Dad?" Lucy said.

"I'm still praying about our situation this fall."

Oh. That was why she hadn't told him. He had way bigger problems on his mind.

"And I know you're still being your Lucy-best."

"I'm on it," Lucy said.

But she wasn't sure she really was. Everybody thought she was Queen Esther all over again. Everybody but her.

J.J. didn't talk to anybody before he climbed into Emanuel's mom's car Thursday morning. Januarie said she didn't know why, and Lucy believed her. She wasn't about to mess with Lucy right now.

When they arrived at camp, Lucy climbed over her to get out first and was headed straight for J.J. when a motor putt-putted up beside her under the cottonwood branches.

"Morning, Lucy," Hawke said from his golf cart.

His sharp eyes smiled right along with his lips, but Lucy's mouth still went dry.

"We need to have that talk," he said. "I'll find you for lunch."

"Okay," Lucy said.

Okay. That was brilliant. If she'd been Rianna, she would probably have whipped out one of those little computers and set up a meeting place. As he drove away, she looked for J.J., but he was already gone.

There would still have been time to look for him, if she hadn't seen something large and red coming toward her.

"What is *that?*" someone said behind her.

Lucy thought it might be Sarah, but she was too busy staring at the big thing to turn around. Somebody was carrying a red card that was bigger than she was. Only the expensive tennis shoes identified her.

As Rianna and the giant red card got closer, Lucy could read the letters painted on it in black: For Anybody Who Brings Soccer Down.

The card stopped a few feet from Lucy, and Rianna stuck her head out from behind it.

"Excuse me. I need to get by," she said.

Sarah stepped aside, but Lucy was still staring.

"Hello—you're in my way."

"What's this for?" Lucy said.

"Like it isn't totally obvious." Rianna gave an elaborate sigh and set the lower edge of the big card on the ground. "This goes to the next person who cheats or plays dirty or basically gives soccer a bad name."

"Who's giving it out?" Waverly had by now joined them and was frowning so hard Lucy could almost hear the lines carving between her eyebrows.

"I am," Rianna said.

"Did you ask Hawke?"

"We're going to be discussing it today at lunch. I eat with him every day—just me and him."

Lucy smothered a smile. There was *another* lie. She hadn't eaten with him the day before, like she said, because Hawke was out patrolling the tables and discovering the mustard incident. And he wasn't eating with her today, because he'd invited Lucy to lunch. This girl was shameless.

"I didn't even know anybody *else* was playing dirty," Sarah said.

"Oh, they are," Rianna said. "But I'm not going to give names."

Because you don't know any, Lucy wanted to say as she headed toward their team's bench.

"Why don't you ask Rooney?" Rianna said.

Lucy stopped.

"Who's Rooney?" Sarah said.

Rianna parted with one of her ugly laughs. "You are, like, the most clueless people on the planet."

Sarah and Waverly looked at Lucy. They did appear clueless—as clueless as Lucy herself felt.

Coach Neely paired them off that morning to practice shielding, turning, and faking. Lucy felt a stab. That was the game she and J.J. had played the day of the storm, way back when soccer was still fun. But when Coach put Lucy with Rianna, Lucy was actually glad. There was something she needed to find out.

When they had their cones set up and were ready to try to score on each other, Lucy took off dribbling the ball. She let Rianna intercept it so she could get behind her. That made it easier to talk near her ear.

"What did you mean 'ask Rooney?'" she said.

Rianna put out her arms to keep Lucy back, which wasn't legal, but Lucy didn't call her on it. "You know what I meant."

"If I knew, I wouldn't be asking you."

Rianna tried to fake to the other direction, but Lucy didn't fall for it. Still, she didn't take the ball, but ran alongside her.

"You know the cheaters," Rianna said, words coming out in puffs as she dribbled toward Lucy's cones.

"I only know one cheater," Lucy said.

"Huh." Rianna stopped the ball, turned, and dribbled the other way. That was supposed to catch her by surprise, Lucy knew, but it was just what she'd wanted Rianna to do. At least until she found out what she needed to know.

"I haven't heard about any other cheaters," Lucy said at her heels.

"Then you aren't talking to the right people."

Rianna made another turn, stepping over the ball and using the inside of her foot to push it back, but this time, Lucy got in front of her, knees bent, legs apart, staying low with her arms out wide.

"Obstruction!" Rianna shouted.

"Containment!" Lucy shouted back, and made her dribble to the side.

"Foul!" Rianna screamed. "Foul!"

A whistle blew, and Coach Neely was on them, sunglasses on top of her head, a sure sign that she was getting annoyed.

"What's going on?" she said.

"Rooney was obstructing me!" Rianna said, still yelling as if Coach Neely were on another field.

"Oh—*Lucy* is Rooney," Sarah said to someone.

"It's only obstruction if you're trying to block your opponent," Lucy shrugged. "I was going for the ball."

"I wasn't watching," Coach Neely said. "But it's just a drill, Rianna."

Rianna turned on the coach, and for a split second, Lucy thought

Rianna was going to smack her. She was sure some of the other girls gasped. Patricia was definitely muttering.

Then Rianna took a step back and slowly folded her arms. "I'm over it," she said.

"Good. That's what I like to see." Coach Neely smiled at Rianna and blew her whistle. "All right, let's change partners!"

But before Lucy could trot off to join Kayla, Rianna stepped in front of her—a clear case of obstruction.

"I know who's going to get the big fat red card if they're not careful," Rianna said, as she jerked her head, splashing her ponytail against the side of her face. Lucy followed with her eyes—to her Los Suenos Dreams.

13

The minute Coach Neely called for the lunch break, Lucy ran straight toward the Los Suenos table. Hawke was going to find her, she knew, but she had to talk to J.J. first. And then she had to get to Hawke before Rianna did with her big red card. Her thoughts were jabbing at her like accusing fingers.

Why hadn't she gone to Hawke in the first place like J.J. had told her to?

Why had she believed that Rianna going for the VIP award—however she could—wasn't going to hurt anybody?

What was all this going to do to her chances at ODP? If she didn't get all of this worked out, she wasn't going to be able to dribble without tripping over herself from the stress.

Queen Esther had it easy compared to this.

Lucy was almost to the Dreams' table when Januarie was suddenly beside her, with Mustard Girl in tow. She was mustard-less and smiling.

"See?" Januarie said. "We're friends."

"Good." Lucy looked over their heads at the table, but she couldn't see J.J.

"Yo-Yo knows stuff," Januarie said.

"Who's—oh." Lucy nodded absently at the chubbier-than-Januarie child. "I bet you know a lot of stuff. I've got to go."

"Stuff you want to know," Januarie said.

Lucy tried to edge around them. "Right now all I want to know is where J.J. is."

"He's hiding."

"Hiding?" Lucy forced herself to give Januarie her full attention. "What are you talking about? Who's he hiding from?"

Januarie nudged Yo-Yo, who said, "My sister."

Lucy was ready to chew through barbed wire to get away, but she looked down at Yo-Yo as she walked. "Your sister got kicked out, didn't she?"

"Not my sister Lawanda—my sister Rianna."

Lucy stopped. Januarie's toe caught the back of her shoe and pulled it halfway off, but Lucy didn't bother to fix it. Her eyes were glued to the moon-face that blinked back at her.

"Rianna is your sister?"

"I hate her," Yo-Yo said. "She's so mean to me. One time—"

Lucy bent at the waist and grabbed her shoulders. "Why is J.J. hiding from her?"

"Because she wrote him a note." Januarie pursed her lips importantly. "Yo-Yo saw her do it."

"What did it say?"

"I don't know."

"But it was probably something mean," Januarie said. "Right?"

Yo-Yo gave a solemn nod.

"You want us to find out for you?" Januarie said. "You know I can always find out stuff."

"No," Lucy said. "Absolutely not—and I mean it. Stay as far away from this as you can."

They looked so disappointed, Lucy stopped again and tugged at both lopsided ponytails.

"You did the right thing coming to me, and I *really* appreciate it."

"Then we helped?" Januarie said.

"You were amazing." Lucy squinted toward the table. "If I just knew where he was hiding."

"Oh, that's easy. He's in the boys' bathroom."

"But I'm not goin' in there to get him for you!" Yo-Yo said. "My sister Lawanda made me do that one time, and it was so gross."

Lucy's heart beat like Mr. Auggy's mad dog. This was going to be harder than she thought, and she still had to be ready for Hawke when he found her.

She looked down at the pair of round faces that were still watching her. "You want to help some more?"

She thought their heads were going to come off, they nodded them so hard.

"Okay, watch for Hawke. He's probably in that golf cart thing he drives around in. When you see him, just try to keep him there until I'm done talking to J.J."

"How do we do that?" Januarie said.

Yo-Yo pointed a chubby finger. "There's your brother."

J.J. was indeed peering out of the boys' bathroom. Lucy charged for the building.

"What do we do with Hawke?" Januarie called to her.

"Just talk to him," Lucy called back over her shoulder. "It's what you *do!*"

Then she left them to figure it out and ran toward J.J. He was still peeking out from the restroom door, and Lucy was almost there when she caught an all-too familiar figure out of the corner of her eye. Rianna was going in the same direction. J.J.'s head disappeared inside the boys' room.

At the same time, Lucy heard the putt-putt sound of the golf cart at the far end of the picnic area. It stopped, and she saw a clump of boys sidle up to it. Lucy's mind raced. She had to keep Rianna from getting to Hawke before she did.

She flipped her head around. Not five feet away was the Los Suenos table, though her friends were hard to recognize. They were all slumped over their lunches, except Gabe, who was savagely pitching tortilla chips into the trash can, one by one.

Lucy flew to the group, glancing back at Rianna who was moving in the direction of the golf cart.

"Lucy!" Dusty called to her.

Lucy put her finger to her lips and looked back to make sure Rianna hadn't heard.

"Guess what?" Carla Rosa said. "I didn't think you were that mean."

"We don't even think it's true, Carla Rosa," Veronica said, and burst into tears.

The boy with the big hair next to her looked bewildered. Gabe made some loud guy sound and stuffed the whole chip bag into the trash can.

Lucy crouched down beside Dusty. The table nearly turned over as they all leaned that way.

"I don't know what's going on," Lucy said, "but I need your help."

"First you gotta tell us if you—" Gabe said.

"Guess what—"

"Everybody hush." Dusty looked into Lucy's eyes. "What do you need, *Bolillo?*"

Lucy was completely confused, but she pointed to Rianna, who was weaving, lips curled, through Januarie's team lined up at the water fountain. "See that girl over there?"

"Yeah."

"Keep her away from Hawke until I get to him, okay?"

"Guess what? We don't know her," Carla Rosa said.

"And I don't think we want to," Veronica said. "Look at her—she thinks she's all that."

Dusty got up. "I'll do it."

"I'll come with you." Gabe wiggled his eyebrows at Veronica. "She's hot."

"No, Gabe," Lucy said. "*You've* gotta get J.J. out of the boys' bathroom. Tell him to meet me behind the building—fast."

"What do I look like—Match dot com?"

"Somebody do it!" Lucy heard the almost-tears in her own voice. "I'm trying to find out what's going on—"

"Yeah," Gabe said. He was suddenly sober. "So are we."

"Then help me!" She looked toward the water fountain where Dusty and Veronica had Rianna cornered, but she knew they couldn't keep her there for long. Hawke was still talking to the boys at the other end, but he'd started the motor up again.

"Please!" she said.

Emanuel untangled his long legs from the picnic table and loped toward the restroom.

"You gotta go?" Oscar called to him.

"I'm gettin' J.J.," Emanuel said.

Lucy took off after Emanuel, with Carla Rosa saying, "Guess what?" behind her, and Gabe telling her he didn't *care* "what." Lucy went to the back of the building and leaned against the outside bathroom wall and tried to hear, but all she could make out was some flushing and some water running and some of that laughing boys always did that signaled they were planning something stupid. She was about to tear her ponytail out by its roots when J.J. came around the corner. He flattened himself against the wall beside her.

"What does the note say?" she said.

"It's not true."

"If it's from Rianna, I know it's not true, but what does it say?"

J.J. dug into his pocket and pulled out a piece of blue paper, the same color as the Fair Play Code. But when Lucy looked at it, there was nothing fair on it. Not even close:

"It has been found out that your team and Lucy Rooney are planning how you can purposely lose in the game with the Select Team and make her look good for the ODP scout——which is the only way she CAN look good. It is well known that if your team doesn't help her, she will make sure somebody gets hurt. She has already damaged someone's ankle on the Select Team ON PURPOSE."

"This means you are going against the Fair Play Code and could get in trouble, especially J.J., Lucy Rooney's main contact, who will be the one inflicting bodily injury. See below."

Lucy looked at the bottom of the page at a photograph of J.J.—fists clenched, jaw tight, eyes flashing fire. She felt the knot in her stomach cinch in.

"I look like my dad," J.J. said.

Lucy shook her head. "Do you know when was this taken?"

"You do."

"No I don't, J.J. You never look like this—"

J.J.'s eyes searched her face.

"Okay, the day Rianna had me by the arm you did ," Lucy said, "but you didn't do anything to her."

"I wanted to. Just like I wanted to tear something up when we were at the soccer field the other day."

They stood there in an aching silence. J.J. poked at the paper.

Lucy read on.

`"There is a way to stay out of trouble over this and not get thrown out of camp. I will find J.J. at the end of lunch today and tell you how. Stay in plain sight."`

Lucy looked up from the page. The paper was shaking. "This is why you were hiding."

"Yeah."

"The team knows about this?"

J.J. nodded. "I wasn't gonna tell 'em. Stupid Gabe got it out of my hand."

"That's why they were acting all weird with me."

"They're just freakin' out."

Lucy scanned the area with her eyes. Hawke was driving along the edge, hand shielding his brow like he was looking for someone. Rianna was peeling herself away from Dusty and Veronica, eyes on Hawke. And Januarie and Yo-Yo were bouncing toward the golf cart like a pair of runaway beach balls.

"Don't talk to her, J.J.," Lucy said. She folded the paper and stuffed it into her shorts pocket.

"Who?"

"You know who—Rianna."

"She made some other girl give it to me."

"That one?" Lucy said. She pointed her chin. "The one with Januarie?"

"No. Some girl from your team. I don't know which one." J.J. shrugged. "They all look the same."

Lucy's heart took a dive, but she didn't have time to go there. The golf cart had stopped, because Yo-Yo and Januarie were standing in front of it, waving their arms. Rianna had been way-laid by somebody. Lucy squinted and felt her jaw drop. Oscar was between Rianna and her destination, chewing his toothpick.

"Stay away from Rianna," Lucy said to J.J., walking backward. "I'll find out what she's up to. Tell everybody I didn't have anything to do with this."

J.J. nodded, and Lucy took off at a dead run.

By the time she reached Hawke, he had a cheek full of something he was trying to chew, and Januarie was pushing a Three Musketeers bar into his hand. Lucy was glad she hadn't confiscated that part of Januarie's loot.

Hawke grinned, as best he could, when he saw Lucy. "I have enjoyed the treat, ladies, thank you very much. But I have an appointment with this lady—who, I think, is responsible for you two being—what was it you told me?"

"BFFs," Yo-Yo said. "Best Friends Forever."

"That's what soccer camp is about." Hawke patted the seat beside him. "Now, Lucy, if you'll just jump in—"

"Coach Hawke!"

Lucy closed her eyes. If she'd just gotten there thirty seconds earlier...

"Rianna," Hawke said. "What's that you have there?"

Lucy turned around. Somewhere between Oscar and here, Rianna had picked up the gigantic red card and was smiling proudly above it. Lucy nearly bit her own tongue off.

While Rianna rattled on to Hawke, and Hawke sat, arms folded and listening, Lucy tried to land on what she was supposed to do now.

Should she just show Hawke the blue paper with Rianna standing there? Tell him she knew Rianna had typed it, and that somehow this was part of her trying to "show him" and get some kind of revenge for her sister?

If she did, what was to keep Hawke from believing what Rianna said on there about *her?*

Besides, Lucy didn't know yet what Rianna was planning to say to J.J.

"I'm impressed with your commitment to the integrity of the sport," Hawke was saying.

Rianna tilted her head and looked at the ground. Any second, Lucy expected her to say, "Aw, shucks." She felt like she was ready to throw up.

"You're two of a kind," Hawke went on.

Lucy felt her eyes bulge. She and Rianna—alike? Please no.

"Both of you have shown me maturity beyond your years," Hawke went on. "Rianna, I'd like to hold onto your red card and use it at my discretion."

Rianna looked like she didn't know what that meant, but Lucy was pretty sure she did. It sounded like he wanted to be the one to hand out the punishments, not some kid. That was a relief at least.

"Now," Hawke said, "I have something I'd like to discuss with Lucy. Would you excuse us, Rianna?"

Lucy felt Rianna go stiff, but she had to give her credit: she didn't scream and pitch a fit the way Lucy was sure she wanted to.

"Sure," Rianna said, and took a reluctant step back.

Hawke patted the seat again, but Lucy felt herself slowly shaking her head.

"Sir?" she said. "Could we meet tomorrow instead?"

Hawke looked down the length of his nose at her. "Problem?"

She glanced at her watch, though she didn't really see the time. "Lunch is almost over, and Coach Neely doesn't like us to be late."

"That hour did get away from us, didn't it?" Hawke said. "Tomorrow, then. Meet me here at the beginning of lunch."

"Yes, sir."

When she turned to go, Rianna was already gone. Lucy would have given up a chance at a goal if she would stay that way.

14

Nobody talked much in Carla Rosa's car on the way home that Thursday afternoon. Lucy thought the other four girls looked as if they were going to pop like water balloons, and Carla Rosa obviously had a "guess what" waiting to burst out of her. But as Dusty told her in a whisper in the backseat, nobody wanted to talk about the soccer mess in front of Carla's mom.

Lucy had a sad thought: they could have talked to *her* mom about this. About anything. That was true for Dad too, but she couldn't bother him. He had something way bigger than this on his mind.

Or was it bigger? Things at camp had gotten so ugly, moving away didn't seem that bad at the moment.

Until the SUV pulled up to Lucy's house and Dusty grabbed her hand and squeezed it.

"I know that paper is a lie," she whispered.

Lucy swallowed back tears and climbed out.

"You girls sure are quiet today," Carla's mom said.

"Guess what?" Carla Rosa said.

As the door closed behind her, Lucy heard Dusty, Veronica, and even Januarie all buzzing her to hush up.

Lucy dragged herself to the top of the back steps before she realized Mudge was meowing forlornly at her heels.

"I'm sorry, kitty," she said as she scooped him into her arms. "I didn't mean to ignore you." She squeezed another mew out of him. "It must be so easy being a cat. I wish I was one right now."

"Uh-oh."

Lucy looked up to see Mora standing behind the screen door.

"Things must be really bad if you're wishing you were feline. Personally, I think you'd look pretty weird with whiskers."

Mudge was now hissing, and Lucy let him go and pushed past Mora into the house.

"What's up with *you?*" Mora said.

"I'm going to my room," Lucy said.

Inez turned from the sink. "Senorita—"

"I don't need a snack, thanks."

"I have the message for you from Senor Ted."

Lucy stopped in the doorway to the hall. "My dad?"

"He says tell you Senor Auggy, he will be here for the reading lesson tonight."

Could this day get any worse? How was she supposed to concentrate on that right now? Lucy let out a sigh that came from the soles of her tennis shoes and then turned again to the hall.

"Okay, take her temperature, Abuela," Mora said. "She doesn't want a snack *and* she's not doing cartwheels because Mr. A is coming. Yeah, she's sick."

"Mora," Inez said—in the low voice even Mora didn't argue with.

Mora shrugged and wandered back to the living room. Inez padded across the kitchen holding something. Lucy didn't see until she was right beside her that it was her Bible.

"Practice the reading," she said as she pressed it into Lucy's hands.

"You want me to read *this?*" Lucy said.

"*Sí,*" Inez said. "The Senora Queen Esther—she can help you." Then she went back to the sink.

Lucy carried the Bible carefully to her room. But once she was inside with the door shut, she set it on the dresser and looked at it from her bed. Lolli jumped from the windowsill and sniffed at its cracked leather cover.

"You can probably read it as good as I can," Lucy said to her.

The first day Inez had started Bible study with her and Mora back in January, she'd tried to get them to read it themselves and had figured out pretty fast that Lucy wasn't a reader. Ever since then, she had always told them the stories instead. A large lump formed in Lucy's throat as she stared at Inez's special book. Inez was trusting her with it, and she was sure she wouldn't understand a word of it.

The bedroom door squeaked open, and a small orange head poked itself in. Marmalade gave an inquiring mew and landed on the bed, where he sat in front of Lucy and looked at her.

"Inez sent you in here to make sure I was reading, didn't she?" Lucy said. "Okay, I'll try it. But don't expect a miracle."

Lucy pulled the Bible from the dresser and placed it reverently in her lap. A piece of paper stuck out of the top, marking the Book of Esther. Inside, another piece said, in curly handwriting, "Begin at the chapter 4, verse 14."

Lucy dried her sweaty fingers on her shorts and ran one of them down the thin, like-an-onion-skin page, the way Inez always did. The Bible had a nice smell, like candles and tea.

When she stopped on verse fourteen, Lucy touched Marmalade's fur and waited for him to purr before she began.

"Okay—'For if you remain silent at this time, relief and de-liv-er-ance'—okay—'deliverance for the Jews will arise from another place, but you and your father's family will per-ish.'"

Lucy looked at Marmalade. "Perish. You mean, like, die?" She shook her head. At least she and Dad wouldn't die if she didn't figure out what to do at soccer camp. But if she didn't, living wasn't going to be that much fun either.

She licked her lips and read on: "'And who knows but that you have come to royal position for such a time as this?'"

Lucy sank back into her pillows. Marmalade gave a loud meow.

"I can't read anymore," Lucy told him. "I don't even get this." Inez said Queen Esther would help her, but what did it mean—"you have come to royal position for such a time as this?" Was it like the whole reason God made her queen was just so she could convince King Hottie not to kill her people?

Lucy groaned out loud. She was starting to think like Morà. She sat up and read some more. " 'Then Esther sent this reply to Morde—' " Yeah, that must be that Mordecai guy, her cousin. Sort of like J.J. was to her. Lucy cocked her head at the page. What if she substituted...

It was a worth a try.

Lucy studied the page again and began. "Then Lucy sent this reply to J.J.," she read to Marmalade. "Go gather together all the Dreams who are in Las Cruces Soccer Camp, and fast for me. Do not eat or drink for three days, night or day."

Lucy looked at Marmalade. "Okay, *that's* not gonna happen." She couldn't imagine Januarie—or anybody else, for that matter—going without food or drink. Even skinny Veronica ate like a truck driver when it came to French fries or Claudia's chocolate soccer balls.

"We'll skip that part," she said to the kitty. "Okay, 'When this is done ...,' here we go. I will go to the king—Hawke—even though it is against the, uh, soccer camp rule about not tattling to him. And if I perish—uh, if I get kicked out of camp, I get kicked out of camp." Lucy stroked Marmalade's back. "That Queen Esther was totally brave. She could have died going to the king. The worst that can happen to me is I won't get to play in a championship game at camp or get seen by an ODP person. There goes my whole dream."

Lucy felt the back of her neck prickle again. It seemed kind of selfish just to be thinking about her own dreams. What about the way the Los Suenos Dreams were suffering? And not just over soccer. This was about her friends—and about people being stupid and mean to them. And about the deep down inside feeling that she had to do something about it.

Even if her soccer dreams died.

After all, there was always the Los Suenos field. Even though she'd been freaked out when she and J.J. discovered what might actually have happened to it, it still wasn't *completely* destroyed. Maybe they could fix it up and get back what they used to have. At least it was still theirs for now—

But maybe not for long—not with "times being so hard." And not with those corporation people being so pushy they would tear it down on purpose and then bribe people for their votes. She bent over Inez's Bible again and read some more. And then she reached for the Book of Lists and wrote:

Dear God — Is This How Esther Would Do This?

Then she read some more and wrote some more and read even more — until the page got hard to see. When Lucy looked up, the sun was dipping behind the mountains. A sniff told her Inez had already cooked supper. And she could hear voices from the kitchen, Dad's and Mr. Auggy's.

She moved a sleepy Marmalade from her lap and headed out with Inez's Bible. She was feeling so much better, she almost rode the yellow rug — until she heard Mr. Auggy say, "I finally got it out of Pasco."

"What's his plan?" Dad said.

"He's decided to sell the café."

Lucy stepped into the kitchen, frozen down to her bones.

"Champ?" Dad said. His eyes groped for hers.

"He's selling it to those corporation people, isn't he?" she said. "That means he's going to vote to sell the soccer field, too!"

Mr. Auggy looked down at the tabletop, but Dad kept his face pointed toward Lucy.

"It looks that way, Luce."

"But I thought he loved our team!"

"It isn't just about the field," Mr. Auiggy said. He nodded Lucy toward a chair, but she stayed where she was, in the doorway, clutching Inez's Bible.

"I don't care what else it's about," she said. "Those people tore up the bleachers and the refreshment stand on purpose, *after* the storm. They did it so we'd all give up — and we can't!" She whipped her head toward the phone. "We have to call the sheriff! We have to tell him that me and J.J. found —"

"Sit down, Luce," Dad said.

"I can't, Dad — somebody has to do something! This isn't fair!"

"Lucy," Dad said.

His voice wasn't stern, but Lucy pressed her lips together.

"If we start making accusations without proof, we're only going to make things worse."

Lucy shook her head hard. "I don't see how it could get any worse, Dad." Her voice was shaking too. "I don't think I can do any reading tonight."

No one stopped her from running back to her room.

And no one heard her make a secret phone call to Mora later that night.

"I need your help with a plan," she whispered.

"Finally, you come to your senses," Mora said.

Before Lucy fell into a toss-and-turn sleep that night, she added one more thing to her List:

Don't think about our soccer field or us moving until THIS problem is solved.

That helped her focus the next morning when she gathered the Dreams behind the restroom building before camp started. She asked Januarie to be there too.

"Okay, team," she said. "We have a problem, and I think I know how we can deal with it."

"Guess what?" Carla Rosa said. "You're not our captain now. You're not even on our team."

Dusty made a loud buzzing sound. Carla Rosa's brow puckered, but she closed her mouth.

"Go on, Lucy," Dusty said.

"And everybody else, hush up." Veronica looked at Gabe. Tears were already welling up in her eyes.

"I didn't say nothin'!" Gabe said.

Lucy pulled the blue paper from her pocket. "Everybody's seen this, right?"

They all nodded.

"Guess what?" Carla Rosa said. "It says you want us to lose on purpose so you'll look good for POD."

"ODP," Gabe said.

"It isn't true," Lucy said.

Gabe squared his big shoulders. "How do we know that?"

"In the first place, you know me—I would never do that to you guys or anybody else."

"You want ODP pretty bad."

"Not that bad!"

"Shut up, Gabe," J.J. said.

Gabe shrugged his meaty shoulders. "What are you gonna do, J-man? Inflict bodily harm?"

"What does that mean?" Januarie said.

J.J. gave her a dark look. "It's what I'm gonna do to you if you don't—"

"See?" Veronica said—and started to cry again.

Lucy put her hand up. More people were showing up for camp, and Hawke's whistle was going to blow any minute. She couldn't leave the whole team having a meltdown.

"There is only one person I know who would even think up something like this." She thought of Rianna's messenger and added, "Maybe two."

"That Rianna chick," Veronica said. "I don't like her."

"Guess what?" Carla Rosa said. "Lucy does. She likes that whole team better than us."

"No, I don't!"

"Who cares?" Gabe said. "You women—you make everything this big drama."

"*We* do?" Veronica said. "What about you? Yesterday you were wanting to go flirt with her."

"You should talk!"

"Stop!"

Mouths closed, and eyes darted to Lucy.

"Look," she said, "we have to forget all that. I'm telling you the truth: Rianna is just trying to bring me down, and I guess she figures the best way to do that is using you."

"I don't get why," Dusty said.

"Because she's mean to the bone." Januarie's eyes were big. "That's what her sister said." She gave J.J. a look. "Sisters know stuff like that."

"That's part of it," Lucy said. "She's trying to save the family name or something, because that was her sister that got kicked out the first day—so she's trying to win the VIP award and be all buddy-buddy with Hawke, and she wants to be picked for ODP bad."

"So do you," Dusty said. "But you aren't doing all this evil stuff."

"Or are you?"

They all looked at Gabe, who gave a bulky shrug. "I'm just sayin'—this whole thing could be a way for *you* to look good for Hawke."

J.J. took a step forward, his eyes slitted down at Gabe. "She doesn't have to do that to look good," he said.

Gabe pursed his lips to make his kissing sound. J.J. took another step. Veronica squealed, and Carla Rosa shrieked, "Guess what? If you fight, you'll get kicked out."

Emanuel stepped between Gabe and J.J., and Oscar put his hands on J.J.'s shoulders and pulled him back. J.J. shook him off, but he stayed put. Gabe's nostrils were flaring like trumpets.

Lucy suddenly wanted to throw up. "Don't you see what's happening?" she said. "This whole thing is ruining our team. I care about getting noticed by the ODP, but it doesn't have to mean we let somebody get away with breaking us up." She hated that her voice was thick, but she pushed on. "Didn't we lose enough already?"

"Are you talking about our field?" Dusty said.

Gabe folded his meaty arms. "That does reek."

"Okay, so see?" Lucy said. "We might never play soccer together again after this—but what if we were never friends again? What if somebody takes us down and we don't try to do anything about it?"

Oscar looked at Emanuel, chewing his toothpick for all he was worth. "So what are we supposed to do? Take this chick out?"

"I'm all for that," Veronica said.

Gabe grunted.

Lucy shook her head. "No. First I have to know that we're all together on this."

Dusty put her hand up. So did Veronica. Januarie squeezed between them, bobbing her crooked ponytail. J.J. nodded. Oscar looked at Emanuel, who also nodded, so Oscar did, too.. That left only Gabe and Carla Rosa. Dusty nudged her.

"Guess what?" Carla said. "I don't want to get in trouble."

"I'm trying to get us out of trouble, not in," Lucy said. "We have to find out what it is Rianna wants from J.J. to keep her from spreading this big lie about me. Then we can turn her in to Hawke because we'll have proof that she's not following the Fair Play Code."

"What are you thinkin' we oughta do?" Gabe stuck his palm toward Lucy. "Not that I'm gonna do it—I'm just askin'."

Lucy let out a long breath. "I have a plan. It starts with everybody—everybody who wants to—praying."

Gabe hissed.

"I don't think we can do this without God," Lucy said.

That got an eye roll from Gabe, and a nervous giggle from Veronica.

"What else?'" Dusty said.

"It's gonna mean skipping lunch."

Januarie let out one of her Chihuahua yips.

"It's not gonna hurt you to miss a meal," J.J. told her.

"Lunch break is the only time we can do this," Lucy said.

"I'll pass out snacks." Dusty nodded her on.

Lucy put her arms out and beckoned them forward. "Okay, listen carefully, because I only have time to say this once."

Everyone moved in. Even Carla Rosa. Even Gabe.

Lucy was sure God was there too.

15

Lucy had two goals to reach before lunch, neither of which had anything to do with a soccer ball. She prayed for both of those goals while the Select Team was gathering and hoped the Dreams were doing the same.

Coach Neely put a cone in the center of their practice area and announced that they were going to play Coneball for their morning drill. The object, she said, was for Bella, Waverly, Patricia, Taylor, Sarah, and Kayla to try to hit the cone with the ball, while Lucy and Rianna played as defenders to keep them from doing it.

"That will be *so* easy," Rianna said, until Coach Neely added that she and Lucy weren't allowed within three feet of the cone.

"That is so not fair," Lucy heard Rianna mumble under her breath. "Why do I always have to be on this side?" But to Coach Neely, she said, with a huge smile that made Lucy think of Mr. Potato Head, "We'll give 'em a good workout, Coach."

Coach reminded them that the drill was a way to practice their passing and off-the-ball movement skills.

"You girls on the outside pass the ball around until you get an open shot," she said, and blew her whistle.

Lucy bent her knees and put her arms out in defensive position and watched Kayla make a nice shoelace pass to Sarah, who dribbled toward the cone. Lucy was closer to her than Rianna, but Rianna crossed in front of Lucy and ran straight at Sarah. Sarah switched directions and went for the middle, where Rianna had left a hole. Before Lucy could get there to block her pass to Taylor, Rianna leaped in and tried to capture the ball. It bounced over the touchline, and Coach Neely blew her whistle.

"Play your position, Rianna," she said. "Talk to Lucy about who's playing where."

Perfect. While Rianna was curling her lip and looking like she had no intention of discussing anything with anybody, Lucy marched over to her and got her face close to her ear.

"I'm having lunch with Hawke today," she said.

"So?" Rianna said. "I have lunch with him every day."

Lucy bit back the urge to call her a big fat liar. "Then it'll be three of us. Are you meeting him by the last tree? I think that's where he told me to meet him."

"Well, yeah," Rianna said. She didn't even blink. "That's where I always meet him."

"Okay," Lucy said. "I wasn't sure."

"It isn't rocket science, ladies," Coach Neely called to them. "Right and left is all you have to decide."

Rianna fixed on the Mr. Potato Head smile and bounded left of the cone. Lucy gave herself a nod. First goal accomplished. Rianna would be waiting by the last tree, where J.J. would find her while Lucy rode off with Hawke. Now for goal number two . . .

That one was harder. How was Lucy supposed to figure out who Rianna's messenger was, when she'd thought nobody on the team liked the girl? All through Coneball, she tried to watch for anyone who might exchange a smile with Rianna, or give her some kind of signal, or even let her have the ball. But nobody even looked at her, and nobody was willing to give her a chance to keep them from hitting the cone.

Coach Neely was almost smiling at them when she called for a water break. "I think you're actually starting to work together," she said. "Which is a good thing. Your first game in the camp play-offs is Monday afternoon, you know."

"Yeah, Hawke showed me the schedule." Rianna lounged against the second row of bleachers. "We're playing that team from Los Suenos. That oughta be like a practice game for us, right, Coach?"

Taylor narrowed her black eyes. "Why?"

"Because I heard they were a bunch of losers."

Coach Neely actually smiled at her, stinging Lucy right through her skin. "I don't think that goes along with the Fair Play Code, Rianna."

"Okay, so I could've said it different—but it's true, right? They're not that good."

Nobody else seemed to know anything about it. Rianna left to go to the bathroom, and Lucy took a long drink out of her water bottle and hoped her face wasn't turning as red as it felt as she tried to read the other girls' faces. She almost choked when Kayla cocked her little bird head and said, "Didn't you come from that team, Lucy?"

Kayla? It couldn't be her, could it? Lucy liked her. She'd thought they were sort of becoming friends.

"The point is," Coach Neely said, "we are our own team now. Let's focus on working that way." Something that sounded like rap suddenly erupted from her pocket, and Coach pulled out her cell phone. "Finish up your break," she said, and moved to the end of the bleachers, one hand over her ear, the phone in the other.

"I bet it's that other coach," Sarah said. "The hot one with—" She looked at Lucy. "—the Los Suenos team."

Was it Sarah? It couldn't be. She'd never made it a secret that she couldn't stand Rianna. Of course, that could be an act...

Lucy shivered, even though the sun was beating down. It felt so cold, not to be able to trust the people she was playing with.

"They're not all from Los Suenos," Waverly said.

"Who?" Patricia said.

"The people on that team. There's that one cute guy named Yen."

Patricia shook her head. "Zen."

"Oh, yeah. I saw him with that one girl." Taylor looked at Lucy. "What's her name?"

Lucy shrugged, but her head was spinning. J.J. had said not to tell them anything about the Dreams, but they sure knew a whole lot anyway. Patricia, Waverly, Taylor. Any of them could be working with Rianna, just because they thought the Dreams were losers. The only person who hadn't joined in was Bella, but, then, she never did. Lucy could almost feel her heart breaking in half.

Coach returned, smiling from earring to earring.

"Yeah, that was Coach Cutie on the line all right," Patricia muttered.

"Where's Rianna?" Coach Neely said.

"Bathroom," Taylor said.

But Rianna didn't hurry toward them from the direction of the restroom building. She came across the field, breathing like she'd just run from Alamogordo.

"Where were you?" Sarah said.

"Talking to my little sister," Rianna said.

"Who's your little sister?"

"She's on the junior girls' team. She's their best player."

Lucy tried not to stare. Could this girl not tell the truth ever? She straightened her shoulders and took a deep breath. No matter how bad she felt about all this, they had to go through with their plan — because somebody who lied like that could do a lot of damage.

"Pick a partner," Coach Neely said. "Each pair gets a cone for a goal. You and your partner take turns firing balls at each other."

Once again, perfect. Or it would be, if Lucy could just decide which girl was most likely to be in league with Rianna.

"Set up a line that the shooter isn't allowed to cross, and each of you take twenty shots on the other. See who makes the most saves."

The only thing Lucy knew for sure was that being Rianna's partner would be a waste of time, and she didn't have much left before lunch. But Rianna was headed straight for her, and nobody else was begging the girl to work with them. Whoever she'd gotten to pass that note to J.J. obviously wasn't doing it because they liked her.

Lucy felt a light flicker in her head, as if the electricity had just come back on. Of course. Somebody was either being forced by Rianna, which was hard to believe in this group, or they had something to gain too. But what was it?

"Be my partner," someone said behind her.

Lucy turned to Bella. She was somber, as always, black braids hanging as straight as her face. Her eyes didn't waver as she waited for an answer.

"Sure," Lucy said. "We've never worked together before. I'll get our stuff."

Lucy hurried to grab a cone and a ball, but her heart was sinking. This was going to be a total waste of time. There was no way it was Bella.

Still, as Lucy stuck a cone under her arm and reached for a ball, one thing did occur to her. If anybody shut up long enough to hear what anybody else was saying, it was Bella. Maybe she knew something about Rianna's plan. It was Lucy's only shot. Lunch was just fifteen minutes away.

For the first five, Lucy just defended the cone while Bella practiced low balls and got about half of them in. Lucy had never noticed what a good player she was. She was so busy diving for the ball, she didn't have a chance to talk to her—not that she knew what she was going to say. "I know you aren't Rianna's evil little messenger, but do you know who is?" didn't seem like a good choice.

When Bella had taken her twenty shots, they switched places. Lucy got as close to the line as she could and pretended to set herself up.

"I like playing with you better than Rianna," Lucy said.

"Who doesn't?"

So she'd been right about that part. Lucy lobbed a ball that Bella bounced easily off her chest.

"She's kind of pushy," Lucy said.

"She hates you."

Lucy gave the ball a spastic kick that wandered right into Bella's hands. When Bella looked up, their gazes clinked together.

"Do *you*?" Lucy said.

"No."

Lucy lined up her third shot while her mind raced. Bella watched Lucy instead of the ball.

"You won't block her shots that way, Bella," Coach Neely called out.

Neither one of them looked at her. Lucy licked the dry off of her lips and made a shot that Bella let pass between her legs.

"See what I mean?" Coach said, and moved on to Patricia and Waverly.

Bella passed the ball back to Lucy, eyes still on her. Lucy could see she was kind of like J.J.: she could say a lot without ever speaking a word. Only she was going to have to, or Lucy was going to be as clueless as ever.

She pretended to consider one shot and then another while Bella kept ignoring the ball and watching her face. She looked like she was seeing everything.

Okay, then. She might as well go for it.

"Did you give my friend that note from Rianna?" Lucy said.

"Yes."

Lucy kicked the ball, hard, and Bella dove for it and missed. She took her time getting up.

"Why did you do it if you don't hate me?" Lucy said.

Bella's face didn't change. "I wanted to see what she was up to."

"Did you?"

"Yeah."

Lucy stared as Bella juggled the ball on her knee. "I can't stop her," Bella said. "But you guys can." She looked at the pairs of girls scattered on their practice area and curled her lip. "You're actually a team."

She sent the ball to Lucy, who rebounded it and smacked it straight into the cone. She didn't know if goal number two had just been scored or not. But she had to believe it had.

When Coach Neely sent them off to lunch, it was all Lucy could do to race straight to the spot where she'd left Hawke yesterday, and not stop to make sure the Dreams were all where they'd promised to be. She prayed and dragged in a big ol' breath. Coming toward her in the golf cart was King Hawke.

"Finally," he said as she hopped into the passenger seat. "It's hard to get an appointment with you. You're a busy lady."

"Uh-huh," Lucy said.

"Working on your skills. Saving girls from bullies. Taming Rianna."

Lucy tried not to let her mouth drop open. Hawke gave her a sideways look as he drove the cart past the picnic tables.

"Don't think I haven't noticed what an interest you've taken in her," he said. "She's a great player, but I was worried about her attitude at first, knowing other members of her family like I do. This is just between you and me, of course."

Lucy had that throw-up feeling again. "Um, sir?"

"You're not comfortable with that?" Hawke said.

"No, I am — but, if it's just gonna be between us, could we talk at that table over there?" She pointed to the empty table and prayed frantically.

"I think that's an excellent idea," Hawke said.

He pulled up to the table and un-pleated himself from the cart. Lucy stole a look behind her as she climbed out too. Oscar and Emanuel were leaning lazily against the pavilion pole two tables down, between her table and the tree. They seemed to be working very hard at keeping their toothpicks out of their mouths. So far, so good.

Lucy sat where she could still see them and opened her lunch bag — but she knew she wasn't going to eat her sandwich. She pulled off a crust and listened to Hawke.

He looked right at her over the top of his nose. Who *wouldn't* listen when he talked? "Rianna's a talented athlete but, like her sister, not a team player. I wanted to see ODP take a look at her, but I was afraid they'd think she played too much for herself. You see what I'm saying?"

Ya think?

"I do," Lucy said.

"But there's been a big change in her in the last two weeks, and I think that's because of you, Lucy."

Lucy was glad she hadn't taken a bite. She knew she would have choked. "Me?" she managed to say.

Hawke sparkled his sharp blue eyes at her. "That's what I like about you. You have special gifts you aren't even aware of. You bring out the best in people without even knowing you're doing it."

Lucy felt as if the seat was sinking into the ground. If she didn't hurry up and say something, this was going to be harder than she thought.

Hawke was grinning. "Feel free to jump in any time."

"Um, well—" Lucy swallowed. She was going to have to be smoother than this. She thought of Dad's voice pouring molasses and Senora Queen Esther going face down before the king. She shot for somewhere in between.

"Sir?" she said. "I don't think I *have* been a good influence on Rianna. In fact, I think I've brought out the worst in her."

"Oh?" Hawke folded his hands on the table. "How so?"

Okay, just like you practiced it with Marmalade.

Lucy took a ragged breath and started from the beginning. How Rianna first suggested flopping. How she tried to cheat in two of their practice games. How she pretended she'd written the Fair Play Code and handed it out just to impress Hawke into giving her the VIP award. By the time Lucy pulled out the blue paper with Rianna's note and J.J.'s picture on it, before she could even get to what J.J. had overheard Rianna and Lawanda talking about, she could tell he wasn't accepting it all as the absolute truth, the way she had so hoped he would. He rested his chin on his fist and stared hard into her face, so hard she felt like she was at the wrong end of a bow and arrow.

"How do you know it was Rianna who sent this?" he said.

"I have witnesses," Lucy said. She turned toward the junior girls' table, where Yo-Yo and Januarie were sitting so close to the edge of the seat, Lucy was surprised they hadn't fallen off.

"Those two?" Hawke said. "Your mustard girls?"

He really didn't miss anything, just like he said.

"Where is this note now?" he said.

"J.J. has it," Lucy said. "He's trying to find out what it is Rianna wants the team to do so she won't tell that lie about me."

"So J.J. is going to come and tell us what she says and that will be my proof." Hawke shook his head. "I'm in a very bad position here."

Me too! Lucy wanted to cry—with plenty of exclamation points. Where was Gabe with that soccer ball? Did something go wrong? Visions of Dusty falling down from the tree, right in front of Rianna, camera in hand, warped through Lucy's mind like a nightmare.

But it wasn't as bad as the real sight of Oscar and Emanuel stuffing their toothpicks into their mouths and chowing down like they were eating beef jerky. The signal. At the far end of the pavilion, Rianna was elbowing her way through startled campers, overturning juice boxes and leaving a trail of disgruntled shouts. She was going to get to Hawke and Lucy them before Gabe did. Lucy's heart climbed up into her throat.

And then a figure launched itself into the picture, obstruction that would have had a ref's whistle blowing for a foul. Bella planted herself in Rianna's path, and she didn't move.

But someone else did. Tearing down the outside of the pavilion was Gabe, with a soccer ball under his arm—the one Dusty had kicked to him. Lucy almost cried.

Hawke was craning his neck, gazing past Lucy. "I see Rianna down there," he said. "Let's get her over here, and we'll talk this thing through."

Lucy closed her eyes and waited. Come on, Gabe. Come on.

Hawke stood up and waved his arm in Rianna's direction. Oscar and Emanuel looked like they were about to swallow their toothpicks. Januarie actually did fall off her bench. Lucy watched in horror as Rianna faked around Bella and made a beeline for Hawke. It was all over.

Until a curly red head popped up next to Rianna. Lucy watched the mouth open. She couldn't hear what it was saying, but she knew Carla Rosa was clearly asking, "Guess what?"

Rianna kept walking until the next words came. Lucy mouthed them with Carla. *You have a booger hanging out of your nose.* While Rianna stopped and wiped frantically at her nostrils, Gabe picked up speed and landed at the end of Lucy and Hawke's table. He was barely breathing hard as he set the soccer ball down in front of Hawke. All that mad dog dribbling had paid off.

"And this is?" Hawke said.

Lucy turned the ball over and revealed a cell phone, taped to it by Dusty's precious hands.

"This is proof, sir," Lucy said.

16

Lucy had never been in Hawke's office before, but she had the whole waiting room memorized by the time J.J. and then Yo-Yo were ushered out and Hawke finished looking at the video Dusty had taken from up in the cottonwood tree on Mora's camera phone. Lucy forgot all of it when Hawke came out of the inner room with a grim look on his face.

"Thanks for staying here," he said. "I know you would rather have been playing a practice game with your team, but I didn't want you and Rianna together until I had a chance to review this."

Lucy had definitely been grateful for that. As it was, she'd felt Rianna shooting bullets into her back with her eyes as Hawke had driven off with Lucy in the seat beside him, before Rianna could even get to them.

But as Lucy followed Hawke into his private office now, she didn't know whether to be grateful or not. Hawke was quiet and still, but she was sure there was anger right under his skin. His jaw muscles were twitching, just the way J.J.'s did when he was holding back a big-time mad.

Hawke motioned her into a canvas chair and sat in another one facing her.

"Do you know what's on this?" he said, nodding at Mora's cell phone on the desk.

"Not exactly," Lucy said.

"It's Rianna telling J.J. he has to mess up every shot she passes to him in the first play-off game, or she will fake an injury and say he purposely inflicted it on her. She seems to think J.J. would get in more trouble than anyone else who got sent off for dangerous play."

"He'd get sent to foster care!"

Lucy clapped her hand over her mouth, but Coach Hawke was already nodding.

"I know about J.J.'s situation. Coach Auggy tells me he's never lost his temper on the field."

"He never loses his temper *any* time. He doesn't want to be like his father."

"And what about this picture?"

"It's not what it looks like! She kept pushing at him, and he was just telling her to go away before——"

"Before?"

Lucy couldn't answer. She'd already said enough to send J.J. straight to Winnie, the State Lady. All this, and she'd only made things worse? Lucy swallowed hard, but the tears gathered anyway.

Hawke looked at the blue paper again. "You know, it's ridiculous really. No one is going to hurt another player on purpose and get away with it. We have refs with eyes like hawks." He pointed to his own. "They can spot that stuff from a mile away. Even if Rianna had come to me with this, I wouldn't have believed her."

"Oh," Lucy said.

"Part of me wishes *you* had come to me right away, before this appeared." He tapped the paper and then put his hands behind his head and leaned back. "But part of me is glad it worked out this way."

"Glad?" Lucy said.

"I think I can teach Rianna a valuable lesson, and not just her, but the whole camp. We're not just about soccer here. We're about people learning to live with integrity." He stood up and motioned for Lucy to do the same. "I'm going to call the Monday awards assembly now. You sit with your team like you always do, and don't say a word to Rianna. Do you trust me?"

Lucy looked at her lap.

"No?" he said.

"I trust you about soccer." Lucy swallowed again and prayed so hard she was sure he could hear it in her head. "But about J.J.—he shouldn't get in trouble for that picture. He was just protecting me—so let me be the one who—"

"Lucy."

She still couldn't look at him.

"I think you've learned a lot about soccer here."

"I have, but—"

"But I think this situation—I think this is the real reason you came." He nodded toward the door. "I'll see about J.J. You go back to your team."

Lucy met them at the bleachers and sat between Kayla and Sarah. Bella was in front of her. Lucy leaned over and whispered, "Thanks."

Bella just nodded.

"So what's this about?" Waverly said on the other side of Sarah.

While the Select Team came up with every explanation from "Coach Neely is announcing her engagement to Seth," to "Somebody got in trouble for kicking a soccer ball out of a tree," Lucy looked over at her Los Suenos Dreams. They were looking back at her, faces full of question marks.

"You tricked me," said the hot breath that went down Lucy's neck. "You'll get yours."

The microphone squealed, and people shushed each other. Everyone was obviously dying to know what was going on.

After his usual call for everyone to yell that soccer was the best—which came out sounding more like "could we get on with it already?"—Hawke held up his hand.

"I've decided to give this week's VIP award early, since we're starting the play-off games on Monday," he said. "Would Rianna Wallace please come up to the platform?"

Rianna didn't even gasp, though several other people did—like most of the Select Team. A low murmur growled through the rest of the crowd. More kids must know Rianna than Lucy thought.

As Rianna inched impatiently down the row to the aisle, Coach

Neely turned around and gave her a thumbs-up. Wow. Mr. Auggy was wrong about her. She wasn't hands-off with Rianna.

"While Rianna is making her way up here," Hawke said, "I just want to remind everyone that the VIP award is given not to the best player in camp. You're all the best, as far as I can see."

Lucy could almost hear Carla Rosa saying, "Guess what? Everybody can't be the best." Lucy decided she would never be annoyed by Carla's "guess whats" again.

"This award," Hawke went on, "goes to players who show integrity. Who refuse to play dirty and aren't afraid to point it out when other people do. Who care more about the team than they do about themselves when they get out on the field. Who aren't as concerned about winning as they are about playing well and fair. And there is one person who fits that description like it was written for her."

He held out his arm to Rianna as she took the three steps to the platform in one. She was glowing and smiling, doing everything but raising her fist in triumph. Lucy felt the whole Los Suenos team knotting their faces at her. She was doing a fair amount of knotting herself. What was going on?

"Rianna," Hawke said, "I thought you might like to have the honor of giving out this week's award to the winner."

Lucy felt Kayla slap her hand over her mouth. Sarah's shoulders began to shake as she smothered laughter. Some other people didn't even try to hide theirs.

"How does that sound?" Hawke said to Rianna.

Rianna's face was still glowing red, but she was no longer smiling. She didn't even seem to be able to produce the Mr. Potato Head grin. Even from fifty feet away, Lucy could see her eyes flashing. If she hadn't deserved what Hawke was doing to her, Lucy would have felt sorry for her.

Hawke handed her a piece of paper and nodded her toward the microphone.

"Rianna, announce the recipient of this certificate."

Rianna stared at it, and for a dead moment, Lucy thought she was going to crumple it up and swallow it. She wouldn't have been surprised.

But Rianna stepped up to the microphone, opened her mouth barely enough to let sound out, and said, "The award goes to Lucy Rooney."

A squeal erupted from the bleachers. A lot of squeals. A whole chorus of them. And cheers. And whistles. Lucy was halfway down to the platform before she realized most of them were coming from the Select Team.

The only person who wasn't at least clapping was Rianna. When Lucy got to the stage, she thrust the certificate into Lucy's hand—and then she grabbed her around the neck and pulled their heads together.

"You are so dead," she whispered into Lucy's ear.

Then she let go and the crowd cheered some more, and Lucy knew they all thought Rianna had been giving her a congratulations hug.

Hawke put a hand on each of their shoulders and pulled them to either side of him. "You two hang out up here for a photo op," he said.

He went into an explanation of how the play-off games were going to work, but Lucy didn't hear much of it. She stood behind Hawke, next to Rianna, certificate clutched in her hand, and tried to think about how proud Mom would be of her, and what Dad was going to say, and Mr. Auggy. But the way it had come about made it hard to smile.

And had anything really been solved? Did Hawke actually think Rianna was going to get the message from this and change her evil ways? She'd just said Lucy was "so dead." That didn't sound like a lesson learned to her.

"You've worked hard this week," Hawke boomed into the microphone. "And you *all* deserve a reward. What do you say to snow cones on the field?"

There was another cheer, and confusion broke loose as everyone charged down the bleachers. Hawke turned to Rianna and Lucy.

"You two wait for me behind the platform," he said. "I'm going to get somebody to take a picture."

What? Lucy wanted to shout at him. *You're leaving me alone with her? Are you crazy?*

"Sure!" Rianna said, and gave Lucy a not-very-gentle shove toward the back of the platform.

Lucy jumped off before Rianna could push her and was barely on her feet before Rianna was beside her. She grabbed Lucy's arm and yanked her against the boards.

"I don't know what kind of lies you told him—"

"I told him the truth," Lucy said. "Let go of me."

"It's your word against mine, and I guarantee you he'll believe mine."

"He already does," Lucy said. Her voice sounded steady and strong, but her insides were in the biggest knot yet. Rianna was pulling her arm behind her back, stretching the muscles so hard Lucy thought they would snap.

"I said let go."

Rianna wrenched harder. "Not until you tell me what you mean by he already believes me."

"Let go!"

"You heard her. Back off."

Lucy tried to twist around, but she didn't have to see to know it was J.J. It was always J.J., coming to the rescue. And getting himself in trouble for her.

"J.J.—don't!" she said.

"No, bring it on." Rianna tightened her grip on Lucy and maneuvered them both around to face him.

He stood just a few yards away, fists clenched at his sides, jaw clenching so hard Lucy could almost hear his teeth grinding. He was like a steel pole—and Lucy begged him with her eyes not to move.

Rianna got her other arm around Lucy's neck and jerked her back. "Come get your little girlfriend. See what happens."

Lucy tugged hard at Rianna's arm with her free hand, but it didn't budge. Hard fear clamped down on her. No one had ever touched her in anger her whole life.

J.J. took a step forward. Rianna was holding her so tightly, Lucy couldn't move her head enough to shake it at him. You can't get involved in this, she told him with her eyes. You can't be like your dad. But he kept moving toward them.

"I'm telling you one more time to let her go," he said.

"And then what? You're gonna jump me?" Rianna squeezed Lucy again until she couldn't breathe anymore. "Let's just see what you do."

Panic seized Lucy, harder than the hands that held her. If she could have screamed, she would have—at Rianna to stop before she died right there—at J.J. to stop before he lost everything he'd worked so hard to be—

But J.J. just kept coming, and Rianna just kept holding on. Lucy flailed her foot, but Rianna avoided her kick and laughed.

"Go ahead, J.J.," Rianna said. "Make everybody believe what I said about you on that flyer."

J.J. tightened his fists—and his jaw—and his eyes. Lucy closed hers.

And heard him yell, "Hey! We need help back here!"

"Oh, so you can't handle it on your own, wimp?" Rianna said.

But J.J. kept yelling for help. It was something Lucy had never heard him do before. It sounded almost like music.

"You got it, J.J.," someone else yelled.

Rianna let go enough for Lucy to jerk her head around and see Mr. Auggy half-running toward them, a camera bouncing from a strap against his chest. Rianna slithered to the ground, grabbing her own forearm and moaning.

"She hurt me! You saw her—she had me by the arm."

"Give it up, Rianna." That came from Hawke, who strode around the platform and reached them in two long strides. He stood over Rianna looking taller than ever. "It might work on Coach Neely, but you won't get it past me. Get up."

"I'm hurt!"

"I said get up."

Rianna straightened and tossed her head, almost slapping herself in the face with her own braid. "You don't know them," she said as she pointed at Lucy and J.J.

"Maybe not, but I know you," Hawke said. "And I have something for you."

Rianna didn't even look scared. Lucy herself was about to disintegrate into a puddle of Jello. She rubbed at her neck and wished Rianna would just run and get this over with.

"J.J.," Hawke said. "Would you do one more thing, son, and reach under the platform and pull out what I left there?"

J.J. did what he said. Lucy almost did melt when he came out with Rianna's own giant red card.

"Read it for us, Rianna," Hawke said.

"No."

"I said read it."

Lucy bit back a whimper. Even Rianna flinched before she tossed her head again and read in a stiff voice: "For anybody who brings soccer down."

"Sounds like this belongs to you, Rianna," Hawke said. "Take it as a going-away present."

He took the card from J.J. and held it out to Rianna. She didn't take it. Instead, she whipped her head around yet again and thrust a shaking finger at Lucy.

"You didn't see what she did to me—I had to hold onto her so she wouldn't attack me."

"Uh-huh," Hawke said. He pointed toward the bleachers. "You wait for me up there."

"No way. I'm going home—and you will hear from my dad." Her voice got thin and cracked. "You can kick one of the Wallace sisters out—but not both. That's harassment! He'll sue you—he'll have you thrown in jail!"

Hawke didn't say a word. He just watched her disappear past the bleachers to the gate, snapping her braid from side to side and spitting words into the air. Lucy backed against the platform and shook inside.

"You okay, Lucy?" Hawke said.

Lucy could only nod.

"She didn't hurt you, did she?"

"No, I'm fine."

"Take a look at her, Coach, would you?" he said to Mr. Auggy.

"You bet," Mr. Auggy said.

Hawke held his arm out to J.J., who handed him the red card.

"No, son," Hawke said. "I wanted to shake your hand."

Lucy watched J.J.'s Adam's apple bob up and down. But the hand he reached back to Hawke looked sure — like he was starting to turn into a grown-up at that very minute.

"You proved yourself," Hawke said as his big palm engulfed J.J.'s. "I'm sorry this had to happen." He turned to Lucy. "I apologize to both of you. If there is anything I can do to make up for this, you just tell me."

"Okay," Lucy said — brilliant as always.

Hawke looked at Mr. Auggy. "I have to deal with something. You'll—"

"I'll take care of these two."

Hawke nodded and strode away. When he got to the end of the platform, he stopped and turned. "They're everything you said they were, Coach," he said. "And more."

Mr. Auggy gave Lucy's arm the kind of examination Dad himself would have given it. And then Dad and Inez did it again after Mr. Auggy had driven Lucy home in his Jeep. She would much rather have ridden with the other kids — not only because she wanted to hear every detail of how they had pulled off the Esther Plan, but because she could have lived without the lecture Mr. Auggy gave her all the way from Las Cruces.

"Things shouldn't have gotten that far, captain," he said. "I wish you had talked to me when you first started to suspect Rianna."

Lucy opened her mouth and closed it.

"What?" he said.

"Um—I tried to talk to you, but you said I needed to go to my own coach."

Mr. Auggy tucked his lips together and nodded. "I'm sorry, Lucy, I really am. I should have listened to you. Next time, make me pay attention."

"How am I supposed to do that? You're a grown-up! Besides—"

"Besides what?"

"I didn't want to bother you when you already have so much on your mind. You know, our soccer field."

Mr. Auggy pulled the Jeep up to Lucy's house and looked at her. The small smile was nowhere in sight. "Let's make a deal, captain: you are never bothering me when you come to me with a problem. Never. Are we clear?"

"Okay," Lucy said.

"It's not just my job; it's my joy. You got that?"

"Uh-huh."

"And it isn't up to you to worry about me having too much on my mind. Like I said, I'm the grown-up."

"Then I can ask you a question and you'll give it to me straight?"

"Absolutely."

"It's still Rianna's word against J.J.'s and mine. Could she make somebody believe we were attacking her instead of the other way around?"

Mr. Auggy smiled his small smile and reached behind the backseat. He pulled up his camera. "Rianna isn't the only one with friends who take pictures."

Mr. Auggy stayed for supper. Inez left with a special nod for Lucy. After Mora inspected her cell phone, she told Lucy she rocked. Inez had a hard time getting her out the door, and she only went after Lucy promised to tell her the entire story on Monday.

That was, as soon as Lucy knew herself. She still didn't know exactly how it had all come together, so the version she told Dad and Mr. Auggy at the table was like a puzzle with a bunch of the pieces missing.

But it seemed to be enough for them. When she was finished, Dad turned his face to Mr. Auggy, and Mr. Auggy looked back at him like Dad could see him, and they had one of those conversations adults had without even saying anything.

"I'm proud of you, Champ," Dad said finally. "And I think you've shamed us."

"I've 'shamed' you?" Lucy said. "I didn't mean to—honest!"

"It's not a bad thing," Mr. Auggy said. "It just means you did something brave and hard, and we should have been able to do the same thing in our situation."

Lucy thought she might know what they were talking about, but she still said, "I need more information."

"We told you we didn't have enough proof to delve further into this situation with the soccer field." Dad tilted his head back, as if he were looking at the ceiling. Lucy knew he was just seeing his next words. "But I think we've realized that shouldn't have held us back from doing what was right. You showed us that, champ."

Lucy poked at her burrito and wriggled in her chair and just generally didn't know what to say.

"So about that award!" Mr. Auggy said. "I think it calls for a celebration—tomorrow night at Pasco's—the whole team." His small smile grew very big. "The grilled cheese sandwiches are on me."

"I thought he was selling the cafe," Lucy said.

"It's still his until they close the deal. He has a few more weeks."

That wasn't long enough for Lucy. She had to talk to J.J. They had to fix this.

17

The sun didn't sink behind the mountains until almost 8:00 on those summer nights, so there was still plenty of light when Lucy begged Dad to let her go see J.J., with a promise to be back before dark.

J.J. was already hanging out at his front gate, as if he knew she'd be coming. He was glaring at the stuff in his yard as if he hadn't been living with it for twelve years and had just noticed it was all there. At least, all that his father hadn't taken with him last Sunday. That seemed like a long time ago to Lucy now.

"We goin' somewhere?" he said.

"Soccer field," Lucy said.

J.J.'s face darkened. "Why?"

"I just want to see it. I want to tell it we can fix it."

He shrugged and lifted himself over the fence light as a hawk feather, but his brows were still stuck together in a frown.

"How come you don't want to go?" Lucy said as they hurried down Granada Street toward the highway. "Too sad there?"

J.J. grunted.

"That's a no, isn't it?"

He didn't even grunt this time, but Lucy let it go. She had to stay focused.

The tops of the mountains were turning orange when they took the curve in the dirt road past the bridge, and Lucy expected to see the bent frames of the bleachers and the refreshment stand casting crooked shadows across the sad field.

But there were no frames.

Now even the metal was strewn about in pieces, like the toys of an angry, bratty child after a tantrum. Lucy couldn't help herself. She screamed out loud. Maybe it was a scream she'd been needing to scream all day—she wasn't sure. All she knew was that she couldn't stop until J.J. picked up a piece of the metal and forced it into her hand.

"Throw it," he said.

"What?"

"Throw it, or you'll never stop yelling. Throw it."

Lucy stared at the metal as she sobbed, and then she pulled it back like she was putting a ball back into the game and hurled it as hard as she could. When it thudded to the ground, the dust around it startled and settled. So did her screams.

"Come on," J.J. said, and he led the way into the mess.

It didn't seem to scare him the way it did Lucy. She wondered if that was because it looked a lot like his front yard. She herself stepped carefully around the random hunks and tried not to put her foot on any bolts . . .

Lucy stopped and squatted down. There were a *lot* of bolts lying around, all separated from the pieces of metal. And the metal itself didn't look any more mangled than it had the last time they were here.

"J.J.," she said. "I think somebody took it apart."

He glanced up from the chunk he was nudging with his foot and gave her a "du-uh" look.

"No, I'm serious," she said. "Not like they did before—like they did it with tools or something this time."

She heard her voice trail off, felt her eyes pop. J.J. didn't look surprised at all. He just stood up, a metal rail in his hand, and yanked it back as if he were going to thrust it like a spear. And then he let it fall with a thunk to the ground beside him.

"So they finally turned you into a wimp."

Lucy jumped at the voice that growled from the shadows of their lone cottonwood. And then she froze. J.J.'s father stepped out with the ugly smile splitting away from his yellowed teeth. He didn't seem to see Lucy. His eyes were on J.J. as he walked right past her, close enough for her to see his jaw muscles twitching.

"I thought you'd wanna pick that up and waste somebody with it," he said, jerking his head toward the metal piece J.J. had dropped. "Somebody messed up your precious soccer field, son. Don't you want make him pay?"

You! Lucy wanted to scream at him. *You're the one who did this! With your evil tire iron and your nasty old tools!*

But she didn't have to. Mr. Cluck was already driving his thumb into his own chest.

"Bring it on," he said. "Don't be a wimp. Fight back like your old man."

J.J. shook his head.

"No? You don't want to fight me?"

"No," J.J. said. "I don't want to be like you."

His voice was like a thread in the wind. J.J.'s father stepped toward him, his hand cupped around his ear.

"I didn't hear that, did I? I didn't hear you say that to me."

He took the last step and pulled back his fist.

"No!" Lucy screamed.

Mr. Cluck whirled around, his eyes wild as they searched the almost dark for Lucy.

"Run!" J.J. shouted at her. "Run like a mad dog!"

His father whipped back toward him, where J.J. was picking up the metal rail at his feet.

"Leave her alone," J.J. said, and this time his voice was loud enough for all of Los Suenos to hear. Lucy stayed rooted into the ground as J.J. swung the rail out in front of him.

"You think you're gonna hit me with that, son?" Mr. Cluck said.

"I'm not your son!"

"Oh, yes, you are. You're my flesh and blood, and you're just like me."

J.J. looked at the rail and he looked at his father, and then he looked at Lucy. His eyes were brave, but they had tears in them. He didn't want to do it. And she didn't want to make him.

"Hey!" she shouted.

Mr. Cluck turned to her, and she pulled back her leg and kicked at the dirt like it was a soccer ball. A spray of dust came up from the ground and caught him full in the face.

"Run!" J.J. yelled at her.

This time she did, away from the swearing voice that split open on J.J. In terror she looked back over her shoulder, and saw J.J. hold out the rail just in front of his groping father's shins. The man ran straight into it and smacked face fist into the ground, barely missing a hunk of his own handiwork.

J.J. let go of the rail and tore toward Lucy, throwing both hands out to tell her to keep going.

Pretend you're going for the goal, Lucy said in her head. That and *'God, help! Please help us get away!'*

She didn't hear the footsteps behind them until they were across the newly-repaired bridge and tearing toward the highway.

"Faster!" J.J. cried.

Lucy nodded, but she could feel her legs slowing down no matter how hard she pumped. J.J. put his hand on her back and pushed her forward, almost into the path of a car pulling out of the side street.

Sheriff Navarra's car.

His tires squealed at about the same time his door flew open. He was out of the cruiser before it came to a complete stop.

"Mr. Cluck—!" Lucy said.

But the sheriff just grabbed them by their arms and shoved them into the front seat of the car and slammed the door. J.J. tumbled on top of Lucy and she had to fight her way up to look out the window. The sheriff stood face to face in the road with Mr. Cluck, hands out to stop him. But J.J.'s father wasn't going anywhere. His chest heaved and his face was the color of the last of the sunset.

"He's the wimp," Lucy said as she started to cry. "Not you, J.J."

J.J. looked away and Lucy didn't say anything else. She just let him blink away his tears.

It took a while to get it sorted out.

There was the full examination from Dad, who, even after going over every inch of her, still wasn't convinced that Lucy didn't have a scratch on her.

And there was the five-million question session with Sheriff Navarra, who made her repeat everything until she was practically hoarse. And then of course there was the lecture about going to the soccer field when he'd told them not to. Lucy managed to tell him that he needed to be more specific about his orders from now on. He didn't seem to appreciate it.

Finally somebody asked him how he happened to be there when the kids were trying to escape from Mr. Cluck.

He planted his beefy hands on his hips and looked at Lucy the way Gabe did sometimes. "Somebody called in and said they heard a kid screaming over there," he said. "I assume that was you."

"Thank the Lord," Dad said.

The sheriff made a huffing sound. "I never took you for much of a screamer," he said.

She wanted to scream right then. With all of the questioning and the grilling and the lecturing, she hadn't had a chance to talk to J.J. alone, and that was all she wanted to do.

But nobody would let her until the next morning. She was up with the sun, and she and Mudge were outside the gate almost before J.J. stopped throwing pebbles against her window. Mudge didn't even growl at him when he came around the corner. It was like he knew J.J. had had enough creatures growling at him to last him for the rest of his life.

"You okay?" Lucy said, though she knew he wasn't. His eyes were puffy, and his mouth looked like he couldn't trust it not crumple on him.

"No," J.J. said.

"He's really gone now," Lucy said. "My dad said—"

"He wrecked our field."

"I know."

"I always knew it."

J.J. slid down the fence and sat miserably with his feet stuck out onto the dirt path. Lucy joined him.

"You knew it was his tire iron that first day?" she said.

"Yeah. And I saw the prints in the mud from his boots."

Lucy thought of the sheriff squatted by the refreshment stand. That must have been what he was looking at, too.

"So he came to your house to get the tools to finish the job last Sunday," Lucy said. "That's why he was all smiling."

"He never smiles."

J.J. parked his forearms on his knees and let his hands and his head hang. Lucy sat up straighter.

"Stop it, J.J.," she said.

"What?"

"Stop acting like it's your fault. It's not."

"He's my dad."

"No, he's not. You said that yourself, right to his face."

"But he is."

"Nuh-uh." Lucy shook her head so hard it hurt. "A dad's somebody that would do anything for you and you would do anything for him. Mr. Cluck-Face might have given you a last name, but he's not your dad."

Lucy wasn't sure where all that had come from, but she was glad it had. J.J. brought his face up and looked at her. There was something like a smile in his eyes.

"Mr. Cluck-Face?" he said.

"Yeah."

"Am I a Cluck-Face?"

"Are you serious?"

He slowly shook his head and leaned it against the fence, eyes closed. Lucy let him be quiet until he said, "Is that true?"

"What?"

"That your dad'll do anything for you and you'll do anything for him?"

Lucy started to simply say, "of course," but the words caught in her throat. That question still had to be answered—by her.

So instead she said, "We have a party to get ready for. Today, at Felix Pasco's. Hey—" She poked him in the arm. "I still haven't heard how everything happened yesterday."

J.J. just grunted. Yeah. They were getting back to normal.

It was the best party ever. Not just because Felix had grilled cheese *and* tacos *and* a whole bunch of extra pickles—*and* let the team pick any ice cream they wanted from the freezer.

And not just because Felix announced that he wasn't selling his café to those *banditos*, even though they weren't the ones who had wrecked the soccer field after the storm *and* that he was going to tell the other shop owners to do the same for these wonderful children *even though* they were a stubborn lot and wouldn't listen to him yet. The tears were a little embarrassing, but the Rocky Road and Fudge Ripple made up for it.

It wasn't even the best party just because, once Felix stopped crying over their table, the Dreams finally got to talk about how they brought Rianna Wallace to justice. Everybody talked at once, but Lucy was able to sort it out—

"I didn't have any problem *getting* that Rianna girl to talk," J.J. said. "She just wouldn't shut up."

"I taped the camera phone to the ball and kicked it—" Dusty said.

"You kicked it crooked," Gabe said. "I'm good, though, so I caught it—"

As the chatter went on, with Veronica smacking Gabe, which meant she liked him again, and Oscar and Emanuel pounding each other, just because they were Oscar and Emanuel, and Carla Rosa saying "guess what" every other minute, Lucy felt like she was getting one long hug—a hug she actually liked. A hug that helped her make a decision.

She clanged her spoon against her soda glass. "I want to make an announcement."

"Listen up, everybody," Mr. Auggy said. He was sitting in a chair backward, looking like he was everybody's dad and proud of it. "What is it, Captain?"

"Hawke said if there was anything that would make up for all the trouble, I should tell him. And I know what it is." Lucy felt her smile spread so big it almost met in the back of her head. "I'm gonna tell him I want to play with you guys in the play-offs—with my *real* team."

The cheer that went up was almost as loud as it was when Lucy won the VIP award. Dusty, of course, had to hug her neck. Over Dusty's shoulder, Lucy saw that Mr. Auggy wasn't cheering.

"Guess what?" Carla Rosa said when they started to settle. "Mr. Auggy doesn't like that idea."

"How do *you* know?" Veronica said.

Dusty started to buzz, but Mr. Auggy put his hand on her shoulder. "It's okay—I think it's a very generous idea. That's just like our captain, right?"

Lucy heard the "but" in his voice.

"But that's going to leave the Select Team two players short."

"So you're telling me not to do it?" Lucy said.

Mr. Auggy shook his head. "I'm just giving you information. Nobody has to tell you what to do."

Dusty gave a big sigh. "Yeah. It's like she always knows the right thing."

Lucy was trying to make a list about that in her Book that night when Dad asked if he could come in. She was glad he was there, because she hadn't gotten past: "Dear God: I Don't Know What To Do" in her Book of Lists.

"Are you in a good place?" Dad said.

"Why?" Lucy said.

"Aunt Karen's back from her vacation. She's coming here Sunday."

"Oh," Lucy said.

Dad's eyebrows went up. "That's it? Just 'oh'?"

"I've got a bigger problem than that, Dad," Lucy said. "And I know you have a really big decision to make yourself, but Mr. Auggy said I should let the grown-ups be the grown-ups and let the kids be the kids. So could I talk to you about it?"

Dad smiled his sunshine smile, for a first time in a very long while. "That Mr. Auggy is a prince. What's going on?"

Lucy told him about her soccer team dilemma. He nodded and made small sounds, just the way he did when he and Mr. Auggy were talking. If she wasn't a grown-up, he sure made her feel like one. There was a lot of that going around.

When she was finished, Dad leaned back in the rocker and let there be quiet for a few minutes. When he spoke, his voice was serious and low.

"How did you decide what to do about Rianna?" he said.

"Well, it's kinda weird," Lucy said, "but I used a story in the Bible that Inez showed me."

"That isn't weird at all." Dad's face was mushy. "You are surrounded by adults who love you and teach you the things I miss."

"You don't miss anything!" Lucy said. "You're the best dad in the world!"

"And I have a lot of help. They'll be here for you if I have to go away."

Lucy nodded, but she suddenly couldn't talk.

"I don't want to move you away from all this," he said. "I do think there's one person who would be willing to come and stay with you if I went to school, but—"

Lucy caught her breath. "You're talking about Aunt Karen, aren't you?"

Dad's eyes darted around. "I haven't asked her, and I won't if you absolutely say no. I know she's hard on you." He ran his hand over his fuzzy summer haircut as if he were waiting for Lucy to explode, or at least try to climb out the window.

But she didn't. Maybe there were just too many other things to do before she had the energy to say absolutely no. Or maybe . . .

"I'm sorry, champ," Dad said. "This isn't helping you with your soccer problem, is it?"

"Not exactly," Lucy said. "But I think there's something that might."

18

"All right, seriously, what's different about you?"

Aunt Karen shook back her shiny bob of dark hair and looked Lucy over for about the thirteenth time since she'd arrived after church. She brought her iced latte to the kitchen table where Lucy was *trying* to read.

"You had your hair highlighted," she said. "That's it."

"No," Lucy said.

"It's blonder."

"Must be the sun."

Aunt Karen took a sip from her glass and studied her some more. Lucy went back to the page.

"You're wearing blush," Aunt Karen said.

"Uh, no."

"That must be the sun too then. I bet you're not using sunscreen."

"My coach makes me." Lucy ran her finger down the page and glanced at her watch. Mr. Auggy was going to be there any minute.

"You definitely haven't improved your wardrobe—although I will say you're getting a cute figure."

There was a pause. Lucy looked up to see surprise in Aunt Karen's long comma eyebrows.

"What? No, 'Aunt Karen, stop it! I hate that!'?"

"I don't exactly hate it." Lucy shrugged. "It's just the way you are."

"All right, that's it. Who are you, and what have you done with my niece?"

"She's just growing up, Karen," Dad said from the doorway. "Luce, I heard Mr. Auggy pull up. You ready?"

"Ready for what?" Aunt Karen said.

"I'm taking a reading test," Lucy said. "You can stay if you want."

Aunt Karen just stared at her. It was one of the few times Lucy had ever known her to be without any words.

And that was good, because in spite of how brave she was acting, Lucy was nervous. This would be her first time reading out loud to Mr. Auggy. If she couldn't do it like a seventh grader, maybe it wouldn't matter what decision she made about which team to play with. That was one thing she was still afraid to ask Dad.

While Aunt Karen made her usual big deal over Mr. Auggy — Veronica would say she was crushing on him — Lucy drank an entire glass of water and still felt dry as the desert itself. When Aunt Karen was finally convinced that Mr. Auggy did *not* want an iced latte, she and Dad sat in chairs away from the table, and Mr. Auggy pulled one up beside Lucy.

"You going to read to me about soccer?" he said.

Lucy shook her head. "I'm going to read from Esther. Is that okay?"

"That is more than okay." Mr. Auggy sat back in the chair. "Take your time, captain."

"Oh — one thing." Lucy pulled Marmalade into her lap. Then she turned to the page.

She read the story of Esther, how the vile Haman thought Mordecai would be put to death so he built gallows for him. How he thought the king was going to honor him, and how the king made Haman give the honor to Mordecai. And how after Esther bravely told the king the terrible things Haman planned for her people, he himself was hanged from the gallows he'd built.

And how Esther didn't go out and fight beside her people, but asked the king to allow them to fight for themselves.

" 'For the Jews,' " Lucy read, " 'it was a time of happiness and joy, gladness and ho—' Oh, the *h* is silent. 'It was a time of happiness and joy, gladness and honor.' " She turned back a few of the delicate pages. "I want to read this one other part because it's my favorite. Okay—'For if you remain silent at this time, relief and de-li-ver-ance for the Jews will arise from another place, but you and your father's family will perish. And who knows but that you have come to royal position for such a time as this?' "

When Lucy stopped, she wondered if everyone in the room had evaporated. There wasn't a sound. Not even Aunt Karen spoke.

Lucy didn't look up from the page. "I messed up some words."

"So do I when I read the Bible. It isn't the easiest piece of literature there is." Mr. Auggy scooted his chair in some more and sat on the edge. "That isn't the point anyway. What I'm looking for is whether you understand what you just read."

"You want me to explain it?" Lucy said.

Mr. Auggy nodded.

Lucy once again ran her finger down the page, the way Inez did. And folded her hands, like Inez did too. And then she knew something Inez knew—something that she'd been trying to show her all along.

"It means if you're going to grow up, you have to do things you don't want to do sometimes because it's right for other people, and maybe you're the only one who can do it."

"Miss Lucy," Mr. Auggy said in a husky voice, "you are officially a seventh grader."

Aunt Karen said, "Well, I'm impressed," and Mr. Auggy smiled his small smile. But Lucy just looked down at the Book of Esther through a blur of tears.

"What's going on, Luce?" Dad said.

"She's about to cry," Aunt Karen said. "Now, how did you know that?"

"Luce?"

"I know what I have to do now," Lucy said in a thick voice.

"About the game tomorrow?" Mr. Auggy said.

"Yeah." She swallowed a big knot. "And—about Aunt Karen."

"What about me?"

Dad was nodding. His unseeing eyes had tears in them too, as if he saw Lucy very, very clearly.

"We'll talk later," he said. "Right now, I think Lucy has some calls to make."

Most of the Dreams weren't happy with what Lucy had to say on the phone. Gabe said, "We got me and the J-man, so what's the big deal?" But Veronica cried, and Carla Rosa said, "Guess what? We'll lose now," and Dusty didn't say much at all.

Only J.J. seemed to get it—maybe because she talked to him in person, since he didn't have a phone. Or maybe because he knew about that "having to do things you didn't want to do because it was right for other people" thing.

After all, he had Januarie.

"I know you guys will be fine without me," Lucy said as they sat on her front steps, watching the Sunday sunset.

"No, we won't."

"That doesn't help me, J.J."

"It's worse for you, though."

Lucy peered at him through the dimming light. "Why?"

"You have to play against your own team."

"That doesn't help me either!"

"You gotta try to win," J.J. said.

Lucy looked down at her hands.

"You gotta."

"I know." She sighed hard. "Sometimes I don't want to grow up, J.J."

"Too late."

"Huh?"

J.J. looked at his hands too. "I think you already did it."

"Hey, I just thought of something."

Lucy looked at Sarah-of-the-long-ponytail, who was crouched next to her in the circle the Select Team had made around Coach Neely.

Coach Neely glanced at her watch. "What's that, Sarah? We only have a few more minutes."

"You used to be on the Los Suenos team, right?" Sarah said to Lucy.

"Uh-huh."

"So you know stuff about them—you know, like, who's a weak defender and who not to pass to—"

"There will be none of that."

Lucy saw she wasn't the only one who stared at Coach Neely like she'd just had a personality transplant.

"There has been enough of that kind of thing here at camp," Coach Neely said. She pulled her sunglasses down her nose and scanned them all with her blue eyes. Lucy had never seen her really look at them before, not like that, not like she really saw them. "We're here to play clean, fair soccer. No 'flopping.' No 'spies from the other team.' All I want you to do is get out there and show that you can work as a team."

So *that* was what that meeting all the coaches had to go to that morning with Hawke was all about. Taylor and Sarah had been *sure* it was an engagement party for Coach Neely and Coach Seth.

But right now, Coach Neely didn't look all fluttery and giggly like somebody's fiancée. She looked like a real coach.

"I know Rianna turned out to be the opposite of Fair Play," she said. "But I want you to remember what she did bring to the table."

"What table?" Patricia muttered.

"'Play fair. Play to win, but accept defeat with dignity. Observe the laws of the game. Denounce those who attempt to discredit our sport. Use soccer to make a better world.'"

Lucy felt her chest puff out. Kayla looked a little taller. Patricia stopped muttering. Waverly actually smiled.

"Now—one question before we go out and warm up." Coach

Neely pushed her sunglasses back up her nose. "Who is going to be our team captain?"

"You aren't gonna pick?" Taylor said.

"You're the ones who are going to be out there listening to her. It should be somebody *you* respect."

Huh. Mr. Auggy was right. She really was a hands-off coach.

"Lucy." Kayla pointed a small finger at her. "I think it should be Lucy."

Taylor snorted. "Who else?"

"Team?" Coach Neely said.

Everyone nodded—Bella hardest of all. Lucy swallowed a huge lump in her throat.

"Good choice." Coach Neely stood up. "Then let's go play some soccer, ladies."

It helped to know that Inez and Mora and Dad—who took the afternoon off—and even Aunt Karen were all in the stands. She said if she was going to be a "soccer mom" starting in September, she needed to get started. Having them all up there, and imagining that Mom was with them, made it easier to stand in the center circle with one of the two refs and face Dusty, the Dreams' new captain. Easier, but still hard.

Because Dusty looked as if she would rather hug Lucy than try to snag the ball from her once the whistle was blown. And the rest of the Los Suenos team was spread outside the circle staring at her like they were trying to figure out who she was now. She still wasn't sure she knew.

"Ready?" the ref said.

Dusty just looked at Lucy. Lucy nodded.

"Then let's play a game."

It felt more like a dribbling drill than a game at first. Lucy got the ball immediately and took off toward the Los Suenos goal with no one on her. She could almost hear Coach Neely saying, *Take as much of the field as the defenders will give you.*

A glance behind told her the Dreams' team was guarding all her *other* players, which meant she couldn't pass. But she could drive all the way to the goal and maybe take a shot on—Carla Rosa? *She* was the goalie?

This was way too easy, and Lucy felt a pang of guilt—until a lanky black-haired figure was suddenly in front of her, one long J.J.-leg ready to capture the ball.

"To me, Lucy!" someone called out.

Patricia had actually opened her mouth to speak, from far down the field. Lucy executed an instep pass that lofted the ball—just the way Coach Neely had taught them. Patricia took it out of the air with her foot and volleyed it right into the goal.

A cheer went up from the crowd, but Lucy couldn't bring herself to join them.

The Select Team scored again before the half, which was really only a quarter since they weren't playing a full game. Still, both sides were sweaty and panting at the break. The Dreams' faces were dragging the ground as they gathered around Seth. From what Lucy could tell, he wasn't doing much to lift them.

"They're actually pretty good at defense," little Kayla said in the Select Team's huddle.

Taylor snorted. "Not their goalie. But, yeah, we should have scored a lot more on them." She darted her dark eyes to Lucy. "No offense."

"Besides, it isn't much of a challenge," Sarah said, "Especially not for Bella. She's mostly just standing down there at our goal by herself."

Bella just shrugged.

"I almost wish this was over," Taylor said.

Waverly gave a somber nod. "Yeah, I kinda feel sorry for them."

"Don't."

All eyes went to Lucy.

"Don't feel sorry for them—they don't want that." Lucy glanced at Coach Neely, who just nodded at her. "This is not telling any secrets or anything, but they've only been playing soccer—period—for six

183

months. They've only been in two real games. They just want to play because they like it."

Sarah flipped her ponytail "Yeah, but they're not trying to get the ODP to invite them to try out like we are. We can't really show our skill against a team that doesn't play for real, and that's all the ODP people want to see. "

"Maybe that's not all," Coach Neely said. "Maybe there's something else you need to show them."

Taylor snorted. "That we can slaughter another team without gloating?"

Hawke blew his horn for the second half.

"Try to learn something from your opponents," Coach Neely said.

"Like what?" Patricia muttered as the team trailed Lucy back to the field. "Just play because you like it?"

Lucy stopped inside the center circle and looked back at her—at the whole Select Team, who could shield and turn and fake, who knew when to dribble and when to pass and when to shoot—and who all looked like it was right up there with getting a tetanus shot.

She turned to Dusty, standing before her, still with a trace of the dream in her eyes—even with a goalie who couldn't catch a ball to save her life and a wing who was too busy deciding which boy to flirt with and a couple of midfielders whose sharpest skill was chewing toothpicks. She and her team still dreamed, even when their field was ruined and their best player was taken away.

The ref set the ball on the ground. "Are we ready?"

"Let's just play because we like it," Lucy said.

"Do what?" the ref said, with the whistle already between his teeth.

"Have fun!!!!!" Lucy said again—and again, until every exclamation point showed up on every face on the field. Every face.

"Now we're ready," Lucy said.

The ref blew the whistle almost before the last syllable was out of Lucy's mouth.

With a lit-up grin, Dusty kicked the ball out of the circle straight to Gabe. "Eat our dust, *Bolillo!*" she said.

"In your dreams!" Lucy said back, and took off after her.

For the first time since the game started, the ball stayed on the Select Team's end of the field for longer than about ten seconds. Emanuel got the ball to the kid Lucy figured was Zen, who did some kind of weird-fancy fake around Kayla and made her giggle.

Veronica called, "To me, Zennie" and trapped the ball he snapped to her. Of course, she took her time trying to set up a shot, and Waverly stole it from her, but Gabe wasn't having it. He got the ball away and sent it rolling to J.J., who went into a slider—and almost got it past Bella. She was down on her knee in a flash, and she gave him a big ol' smile as she kicked the ball far down the field.

"Sorry!" Lucy heard Bella say before she took off again for midfield.

"No problem," J.J. said back.

Lucy felt herself grinning. This was the soccer she loved.

Back on the Los Suenos end, Dusty was running beside Patricia as she dribbled. Only Oscar stood between her and the goal.

"Wall!" Lucy shouted to her as she came even with her on the other side of the field.

Patricia passed the ball off to her and ran around Oscar. He would follow the ball—that was just Oscar—and Lucy could pass it back to Patricia for another score. But to Lucy's surprise, Oscar spit out his toothpick and stayed on Patricia, grinning wide and saying something that got a big ol' guffaw out of her.

Which left Lucy with the ball, and a chance to score. And not just a chance—a sure thing. With the rest of the Dreams guarded, Lucy checked out Carla Rosa. She was far over to the right, watching Oscar and Patricia instead of the ball. All Lucy had to do was aim for the left edge and she was in.

Lucy dribbled closer and set up for an instep shot. And then, suddenly, there was Carla Rosa, throwing herself at the ball, arms out as if she were coming in for a landing. It smacked into her chest and bounced off and out of the goal box.

"Way to go, C.R.!" Gabe shouted.

Lucy was so caught off guard she almost forgot to go for the rebound.

"Behind you!" Taylor said.

Lucy made a heel pass. Gabe was right there to capture it from her. Kayla swooped in like the "smokin' defender" she was, laughter bubbling over happy calls of, "To me, Kayla!" and "Man on!"

The "man on" was Emanuel, who got the ball back down the field to J.J. With one of his best dust-blowing sliders, he sneaked the ball past Bella. Lucy didn't know which team cheered louder.

The whistle blew to end the game. Select girls and Dream kids were in a puppy pile in the middle of the field, when Lucy heard a voice boom, "Lucy Rooney!"

J.J. got her to the top of the heap, and Hawke pulled her out.

"Got something for you and your dad to sign," he said as he ushered her toward the bleachers.

"What?" Lucy said.

"Your application to officially try out for ODP."

Lucy stopped just short of the still-cheering bleachers and stared up at him. "They want to see me?"

"I've already seen you." Hawke's eyes were twinkling. "I'm the ODP rep, Lucy."

Lucy could only stare at him.

"I knew your skills were there the first day I saw you," he said. He looked out at the pile still laughing and shouting in the middle of the field. "But today I found out what I *really* needed to know." Hawke's bright, sharp eyes came back to her. "Your tryout is in September."

Dear God:

Why It's Okay That This Isn't the Perfect Summer

She stopped and rearranged the two cats on her lap. Lolli muttered at Marmalade under her breath, Patricia style, but the orange kitty hunkered down. This was like reading, and that was his job. Lucy picked up her pen again:

1. I still have to take a standardized reading test if I want to be in regular classes when middle school starts — with Dusty and Veronica and Gabe. But Mr. Auggy says I'll pass, no problem, and that I can probably help J.J. too. I don't know about him holding a cat though.

2. Now that soccer camp is over, Januarie is back to hanging out with us. But she isn't as annoying as she used to be. Maybe that's because her team won the junior championship. She was a pretty good goalie for them. She yelped like a Chihuahua at anybody that tried to score a point.

3. The Girls' Select Team didn't win our championship. The Boys' team beat us by one goal. But the whole Los Suenos Dreams Team AND the Girls' Select Team got VIP awards for showing the camp what real sportsmanship is. Huh. All we did was have fun.

Lucy wrote 4, and felt her throat get thick. This was the hardest one, the one that made her almost cry every time she thought about it.

4. Aunt Karen is going to work from here for six weeks while Dad is at that school in Albuquerque, and even though I know she can't change me, I know she's still going to try. It's hard to make THAT part of "un-perfect" an okay thing.

Lucy sank against her pillows and listened to Inez padding around in the kitchen, making breakfast for Lucy and Mora. Aunt Karen was already calling Lucy every day, telling her how she was going to "help" her redecorate her room—which she liked just fine the way her mom had done it when she was five—and get involved with the other "soccer moms"—which Lucy didn't even know they had—and have all Lucy's friends over for a themed sleepover — which — what *was* that anyway?

Lucy pushed the kitties off her lap and tucked the Book of Lists under her pillow and wandered out into the kitchen. Inez looked up from the scrambled eggs she was piling into tortillas as Lucy slumped into a chair.

"You are *triste?*" Inez said.

"Does that mean depressed?" Lucy said.

Inez slid a plate in front of her on the table. "*Sí*. And you are this way because ... Senorita Karen?"

"How do you know, like, everything I'm thinking?" Lucy said.

"I was the young woman once — like you — and Senorita Esther."

Lucy poked at a scrambled egg, wrapped snugly in a tortilla. "I don't think I'm exactly a 'woman,' Inez. If I was, I wouldn't have to have Aunt Karen come and stay with me."

"But you are almost," Inez said. "You are three things a girl must be to become the woman." She held up a brown finger. "Senorita Ruth?"

"I love somebody more than I do myself," Lucy said.

Another finger went up. "Senorita Rachel?"

"I forgave something that seemed like it couldn't be forgiven."

"And what do you do now, that Senora Queen Esther has teached you?"

Lucy got up on one knee. "You mean, 'such a time as this?'"

"*Sí* ..."

"I did something I didn't really want to do because it was the right thing to do and I was the only one who could do it." Lucy took a breath. "So — that wasn't just about soccer."

"No."

"That was about putting up with Aunt Karen so Dad can go to school and not get fired. But I still —"

Inez nodded. And then she smiled and put her lips close to Lucy's ear and whispered, "But no one says that you must like it."

Lucy smiled. And she nodded back. And she felt better.

Maybe not about Aunt Karen. But definitely about being an almost-woman.

Definitely.

WHO HELPED?

Lucy's Perfect Summer is fiction, which means I mostly made it up. But I wanted it to be real too, so I got a lot of help from people who know things I was clueless about—like how to play soccer and what it's like to be a tomboy. I thought that since you are now part of Lucy's team yourself, you'd like to know who the other players are.

Jessica Moose, Elle Rickman, Danielle Cedalles, Kelly Hainline, and Madeline U'Ren are middle schoolers in Alamagordo, New Mexico. They told me all about what it's like to grow up in the southern part of New Mexico and even let me come to their school without being too embarrassed by me. They were awesome.

Hannah Wathne is a twelve-year-old friend of mine who helped me "find" Mora by taking me into the world of dance and girly-girlness. She even has an electronic diary. Hello! How cool is that?

Haili, Caitlin, and Brianna Shubert are ten-year-old sisters (they happen to be triplets!) who took me out on the soccer field and taught me everything they could. It was hard work since I am not athletic and played about as well as Januarie. Maybe a little worse. They were patient and kind, not to mention fun, and I rewarded them with a trip to the mall.

When I went to New Mexico to discover Lucy's world, **Robin Wolf, Doreen Owens, Heather Carter, Linda Castorina and Madeline U'Ren** were my research buddies. They took me everywhere I needed to go, fed me the best Mexican food on the planet, and shared in the squeals when I found just the right details. They loved Lucy before I wrote the first word about her.

We want to hear from you. Please send your comments
about this book to us in care of zreview@zondervan.com. Thank you.

ZONDERVAN.com/
AUTHORTRACKER
follow your favorite authors